Worship
in the Storm

First Published 2019 Tomi Arayomi Ministries

www.tomiarayomi.org

Printed in Great Britain by Biddles Books Limited, King's Lynn, Norfolk

Contents

Acknowledgements

With special thanks to Rachel Yarworth for your laser sharp editing and constant encouragement and for the many hours you poured into this book, it wouldn't have happened without you.

Thanks to Tomi Ayaromi for your wisdom, inspiration, cover design and over all help in getting this book printed. You are a true General of God.

Thanks to my Father in heaven who never leaves me even in the darkest moments of my life.

> *If I ascend into heaven, you are there; If I make my bed*
> *in hell, behold you are there*
>
> *Psalm 139:8*

Commendations

I have known Ali for over twenty years, both as co-minister and good friend. Reading this is like having him walk into a room, pull up a chair and have a good natter, sharing his hard-earned wisdom in an easily accessible way.

It's not a dry manual full of theory but rather a life-bringing overflow of the Biblical principles that he has learned and lived and proved to be true – Biblical principles that will powerfully equip Christians everywhere to see God's victory over the storms in their lives.

Rachel Yarworth – Worship Leader & Senior Leadership,
Cornerstone Family Church, Stourport-on-Severn

I have just finished reading some portions of this new book and I encourage others to read it. I believe what you are going to get out of it is a journey of where we are in praise and worship right now and actually where praise and worship is going. And so it has a strong prophetic edge that goes along with it. I believe you will be blessed by it if you are a worship leader or part of the worship team but I believe that everybody is going to be encouraged, helped and aligned by this book

Dr Sharon Stone –
Director Christian International Europe

I read Ali's book during a personal time of intense warfare. The truth and the wisdom within each chapter certainly poured fuel on the burning of my own heart. Ali is a champion of breakthrough and victory. A man who refuses to tolerate defeat, settle in sin, live less than a full pursuit of 'more' and a man who burns to see others burn too. With Ali what you see is what you get. No professional, false humility or air of importance. Just a real man, living a real walk with God and zealously attacking the enemies of the spirit.

Buy it, read it, apply it and pass it on. This book really will empower you to break out of comfort and apathy and into the real battleground of the spirit using the greatest weapon given to us. Worship!!

Rob Joy –
Director and Founder of Kingdom Cause

Dedication

For my Mum Jenny Loaker, who has always fought for me and stood with me through every storm I have ever faced. A true woman of God.

Introduction

We all go through storms in life. I'll never forget my first one. I was seven years old and it was the summer holidays. I was playing in my friend's garden and messing around with his dog. When I bent down to stroke it, it jumped up and bit me on the face. I remember feeling a sharp pain on my cheek – the same pain you feel when you are injected with a needle, followed by a dull throbbing sensation. I began to feel slightly dizzy and remember seeing the look of horror on my friend's father's face as he swept me up in his arms and carried me to the kitchen table. He was panicking and saying everything was going to be alright. He placed a large white towel over the side of my face and I remember watching it turn red in front of my eyes. I reached up to my face to see if I could feel the wound but remember my hand disappearing into my cheek and touching my teeth.

I had twenty-three stitches in my face that day. The hospital staff gave me lots of money for bravery because, out of curiosity, I insisted on staying awake for the whole operation so I could watch them sow my face up. I bought Kermit, Scooter and Animal, cuddly toys from The Muppets with the money. At that time I had a very innocent relationship with a girl at school which mainly involved being invited to each other's houses to eat jelly, and a little kiss every now and then. When I returned to school, as soon as she saw my face she ran away saying that I looked like a monster. She never invited me around for jelly again.

You may wonder why I have chosen to tell this story in a book which is primarily about worshipping God. The reason is simple, I wanted to illustrate that life is never straight forward for any of us and that storms come to us all, including the author of this book.

Life is full of good days and bad days, dry seasons and fruitful seasons, light and dark.

I wish it wasn't don't you? There are some days that I wish I could just live over and over again because the memory of them is so golden and the beauty of them never fades away. I hear a piece of music and it takes me back to the very spot where I first heard it. I smell a certain smell and it's like I'm there all over again. I'd love to be able to bottle those days and relive them whenever I need to be reminded of how much fun life can be. I usually play "Crazy for you" by Madonna if I want one of those moments: it takes me back to a very special golden summer in my teenage years.

Wouldn't it be good if life was just a constant stream of great experiences and happy memories? When you are young you are full of hopes and dreams of what your life will bring. Sometimes there are seasons where everything seems to be perfect in every way and your greatest dreams are being fulfilled. It's easy to worship God in those seasons because everything is going so well. It's easy to wish those seasons would go on forever but for the vast majority of us that simply isn't the case. At some point summer ends and the darkening wildness of autumn descends upon us. We find ourselves in a storm that can sometimes feel overwhelming. Our world starts crumbling around us and everything we once trusted and relied on is pulled from under our feet. Marriages end, loved ones die, businesses go bankrupt, jobs are lost, health suffers and people we once called friends become enemies. The list of broken hearts and broken dreams is endless. It can feel like a sea voyage where one day the sea is calm and tranquil, but the very next day you are fighting for your life in a huge storm that threatens to sink your ship.

As I write this book I am facing one of the biggest and most fierce storms of my life and these pages are littered with my tears and the cries of my own heart. I have a picture on my wall of a dark violent storm at sea. In the middle of the storm, tossed and thrown around by the huge waves, is a tiny boat. Sometimes I feel like that boat, helpless in the middle of a great ocean and at the mercy of the giant waves.

As Christians we don't like the idea that bad things can happen to good people, yet the Bible is full of stories of how great men and women of God prevailed in the face of terrible adversity. We don't often hear teaching on how to live victoriously in the midst of pain. It's not popular and it doesn't fill seats.

So many good, faithful, beautiful people are destroyed by the storms of their lives because they do not know how to fight when the waves begin crashing in. So many Christians find that at the critical moment they have no strong foundation to stand on of their own. They have built their lives on sinking sand rather than solid rock. They know the best praise and worship albums, the most anointed preachers and the best conferences to go to but they don't know what to do with grief, loss, addiction, pain, sickness, failure, poverty and injustice. They don't know how to stand on the firm promises of God and declare victory in the midst of darkness. We need to be people who are grounded in the Word of God, who know how to walk on the water in the midst of the storm by using the spiritual weapons at our disposal.

Worship is one such weapon.

I truly believe we have entered a new season in the body of Christ where God is building an army that can stand and fight against the enemy during the storm. I believe worship will be instrumental (pardon the pun) in that. In my years of leading worship I have found that praise and worship is one of the most powerful tools we have in the storm. Both in my private devotional life and in public ministry I have witnessed the power of worship to overcome adversity and destroy the works of the devil. I have seen how praise and worship can change the atmosphere and bring about victory over seemingly hopeless situations and impossible odds. Worship is so much more than just singing routine songs on a Sunday morning.

This book is designed to inspire you to experience victory over adversity in your life through praise and worship. Rather than being dry theology it is a road map to triumph, full of the principles I have seen work in my own life and stories that will inspire you to success in your life. You are in covenant relationship with the One who has power over the wind and waves. You are not at the mercy of the storm, the storm is subject to your Father in Heaven! He has plans to give you hope and a future (Jeremiah 29:11); He will see you through. I don't know what storm you are going through right now but what I do know is that every storm must bow at the name of Jesus. If you feel defeated, if you feel like giving up, if the storm seems overwhelming to you and all you can do is curl up in a ball and cry, I want to encourage you today. You are closer to breakthrough in your life than you ever dared believe, you are closer to victory than you ever dared imagine. It's always darkest before the dawn but then the light pierces the darkness. Be encouraged! It's time to walk on the water, let worship guide your steps and let praise be a mighty sword in your hand!

CHAPTER 1

Songs of the Broken

*"Weeping may endure for a night
but joy comes in the morning"*

Psalm 30:5

I was intending this chapter to be the last in the book but I felt compelled by the Holy Spirit to put it first.

If you feel broken, like you can't go on, this chapter is for you. I believe the Lord wants to minister to you as you read and begin a healing process in your life. It is no coincidence that as I write this chapter there is a literal storm raging outside my window. The sky is dark, the wind is powerful and the rain is beating down on this little upper room where I am sitting. Sometimes we come to a place where we feel so broken that it shipwrecks our faith. Something inside us dies and the pain we feel inside becomes all-consuming, like a relentless storm battering our heart. You want to fight, you want to be free, but it feels like the darkness has consumed you and you no longer care whether you live or die. God sees this and I believe He wants you to express it to Him. Sometimes He just wants to sit with you in your brokenness and cry with you. Being in faith to be healed doesn't mean you cannot express how you are feeling inside. In fact that's a great place to start.

I came to the end of myself towards the end of last year. Some things had happened in my life which left a deep wound in me. To everybody else I looked fine from the outside but inside I was dying like a drowning man in an ocean of despair. I am sure my situation isn't anywhere near as severe or painful as some out there but it was significant to me. I would love to say that I fought my way through it in faith but the truth is, to begin with all I could do was sit on my bed and cry. I would sometimes say the word "Jesus" over and over with the tears rolling down my face. I buried my face in a pillow and acknowledged that I was powerless in my own strength to change the situation – only the power of God would bring me through. My prayers mainly consisted of me crying out the Name of Jesus until in the end I would shout it like I was standing on top of a mountain bellowing into the wind. I had to get to a place where I totally surrendered to him and came to the end of myself. Only He could save me from the storm all around me, I had to lean on him completely and trust in Him. As a husband, father, worship director and church pastor, during this time I not only had to carry on preaching but I also had to lead people in worship, lead a team of musicians, lead my church and take care of a family with four children. At times it seemed as if hopelessness and depression would consume me but I just kept going, choosing to believe in and declaring the goodness of God. Many of the worship songs I sang in that time were about the goodness of God. In my brokenness I lifted my hands and worshipped; in my brokenness I declared God to be a good Father, worthy of worship no matter what the circumstances looked like around me. There is something about the songs of a broken person that exude spiritual power. There is such strength and faith in them, there is something resolute and iron in them that declares, "No matter what life throws at me I will still praise you"

God responds to that kind of faith. There is something so powerful about a person who is not defeated by circumstances. I think God honours and draws near to that kind of spirit.

King David knew this, he knew the power of somebody with a broken heart who was still determined to worship:

*"My sacrifice, O God, is a broken spirit; a broken and
contrite heart you, God, will not despise"*

Psalm 51:17

I don't know what you have been through or what you are going
through right now but God is saying to you:

*"Pick yourself up from the ashes, just begin to worship Me; sing,
O barren, declare My Name and watch Me perform miracles in
your life".*

Even if all you can do right now is cry and whisper "Jesus", He
will work with that; He will draw near to you. If you are feeling
angry and frustrated just begin to shout His Name! Cry out
"move, in the name of Jesus!" to the mountain that is in your way
and watch it move. Declare His goodness and praise His Name
over the impossible situation and see His deliverance come to pass.
Sometimes you just have to shout! Sometimes you just have to get
sick and tired of being sick and tired. Look at blind Bartimaeus
in Mark 10:46-52 – he didn't care what people thought, he was
too desperate for that! He had suffered in darkness too long and
he desperately wanted to be able to see. The Bible says that many
people told him to be quiet but he just shouted even louder. He
had come to the end of himself: it was do or die; now or never.
He heard Jesus passing by and he knew this was possibly his
last chance to change his situation. All protocol went out of the
window, all pleasantries and politeness were thrown to the wind;
he was determined to get his miracle and nobody was going to
stop him! What did he shout? What was his first word?

"Jesus!"

Mark 10:47

For a blind beggar, to be able to see would not only be a miracle
but it would also be a complete change of identity. It would mean

no more begging, it would mean dignity restored, it would mean a second chance in life, maybe the chance to earn a living, get married, have children and leave a legacy and an inheritance for generations to come. Maybe you have come to the end of yourself? Maybe your life is in tatters? Maybe your dreams are finished? Maybe you have finally realised that you can't change this situation in your own strength? You are in the hands of the Lord, the master potter, the great I AM. What is fascinating to me about the story of blind Bartimaeus is that when Jesus finally stood in front of him he asked:

"What do you want me to do for you?"

v51

Jesus knew very well why he was there, but He wanted to hear Bartimaeus declare it for himself as a statement of faith. Maybe a loved one has died? Maybe your marriage has come to an end and you have to say goodbye to somebody you've shared your life with for so many years? Maybe you have an addiction that is destroying your life and robbing you of everything you have ever loved? Maybe you have been diagnosed with a terminal illness? Maybe you've lost your job or your business? Maybe your debts are crippling you? Maybe you are unwell or in pain? Jesus is asking you:

"What can I do for you?"

As you worship Him and lift up His name in praise, tell Him in faith what He can do for you; place your destiny in the hands of the Master and see where that takes you. It took Bartimaeus from being a beggar at the side of the road, scorned and frowned upon by society, to being a follower of Jesus rejoicing as he went along the road with Him. Do this and you will have a testimony to share, a song to sing and an unshakeable faith.

4

There is a popular and famous song called "It Is Well with My Soul". Many have sung it but not many know the story behind it:

Horatio G Spafford was a successful businessman with a lovely wife, Anna and four lovely daughters. After a business trip to Chicago he had to stay behind to sort out some unexpected business affairs whilst his wife and daughters travelled home to Europe ahead of him. Roughly four days into the crossing the ship carrying Anna and the girls collided with another ship, placing the passengers in great danger. Anna knelt down on the deck of the ship with the girls and prayed for God's protection and that His will be done. A little while later the ship sank beneath deep waters of the Atlantic, carrying most of the passengers with it, including the four girls. Anna survived but had to live with what had happened for the rest of her life. She sent Horatio a now famous telegram which simply read:

"Saved Alone".

She later said of the incident:

"God gave me four children, now they have been taken from me. Someday I will understand why."

On hearing the news the heartbroken Horatio booked the next boat home to join his wife. It is said that as he passed over the place where the girls had gone down he wrote the now famous song. Was he bitter? Did he blame God? Let's look at some of the words of the song:

"When peace like a river attendeth my way
When sorrows like sea billows roll
Whatever my lot, Thou hast taught me to say
It is well, it is well with my soul"

It is well with my soul. He had purposed in his heart that whatever came his way in life he would not lose his faith in God. I recently read of another famous evangelist called Mary Woodworth Etter who lost five of her six children to sickness but still went on to serve God in a mighty harvest of souls with signs, wonders and miracles wherever she went. It is said of her that she often used to sing during her sermons. The songs of the broken are powerful. Don't let your situation define you, use your experience to lean on Jesus and see what song and testimony comes from your life. Horatio Spafford is gone now but his song still lives on; this song of a broken-hearted man who refused to give up on God is now part of the legacy of his life. When people think of him they don't think of a broken man who was defined by a terrible incident, they think of a faith-filled man who was defined by his relationship with God.

We don't have all the answers, we don't always know why bad things happen. One day we will know all the answers and every tear will be wiped away, but for now it is not our place as the clay to question the potter. Rather we can let Him fill our broken hearts with a new song and mould us into something beautiful to light up the world for his glory. Do I have the answer for the situation that tore my world apart last year? No. I am still walking through it; I am still in the storm but I can tell you that I have many more songs now, many more testimonies and many more reasons to thank God for the amazing breakthrough He has given me during this time. We have a Father in Heaven who understands our suffering; He sent his own Son to die on a cross for us. In the Bible most of the disciples were martyred, John the Baptist was beheaded, innocent children were massacred by King Herod, David's son died and another son betrayed him, Job lost everything, and in Lamentations women even ate their own children to survive! The list goes on. There are also many modern day situations we could compare to some of those mentioned above. Christians are being raped, beheaded and martyred all over the world right now simply for believing in Jesus.

I don't have all the answers and I'm sure we will only know some things when we get to heaven but I have purposed three things in my heart no matter what the circumstances and I would urge you to do the same when you worship. Those three things are:

God is good
Jesus is Lord
The Devil is a liar

Allow yourself to grieve, allow yourself to fully experience the pain you are going through, and then let your Heavenly Father come and lift you out of the pit, set your feet upon a rock and put a new song in your mouth. A song of breakthrough and restoration.

As you sing this new song, do it in faith and hope because even though you might be in the middle of a storm right now, God ultimately has the victory over the storm.

CHAPTER 2

The Battle

"Those who are with us are more than those who are with them"

2 Kings 6:16

Before the next chapter on how worship can be a weapon in the storm I need to lay a simple foundation:

THE BATTLE BELONGS TO THE LORD

It is so important for you to grasp that you do not fight alone and that God Himself fights on your behalf. You cannot defeat the storms of life in your own strength.

In 2 Kings 6 we find Elisha with his servant Gehazi, surrounded by a great army. It turns out that Elisha had seriously angered the King of Syria by telling his enemy the King of Israel everything he was saying in the secrecy of his own bedroom, which included his intended plans for battle. What a handy guy to have around! Elisha gave the king of Israel a massive tactical advantage because of his prophetic insight from God which angered the Syrian king so much he sent an army down to where Elisha lived and surrounded the city with the express purpose of capturing him and maybe killing him.

Now I don't know about you but if I woke up one morning to find my whole town surrounded by a huge army who were there just for me I wouldn't be thinking about what to eat for breakfast! That is what happened to Elisha and his servant. When Gehazi went outside, he looked up to find a great army encamped around them and panicked, asking Elisha what on earth they were going to do to get out of the situation? Elisha's answer is illuminating for us all:

> *"Do not fear, for those who are with us are more than those who are with them"*

v16

Those who are with us are more than those who are with them? Really? Elisha had the revelation that God would fight the battle for him, he knew God would not forsake him and he knew that God was all powerful in this situation. The truth is, if God is for us who can be against us? (Romans 8:31). Elisha's servant must have wondered what Elisha had been smoking when he poked his head outside once more and saw all the multitude of soldiers, horses and chariots waiting to attack. The thing is, he was looking in the natural realm where things always look very different to how they look in the spiritual realm. He needed to have his eyes opened to the reality of what was *really* happening. Elisha then prayed that Gehazi's eyes would be opened to the spirit realm and that he would see the reality of the situation. Gehazi looked again and to his wonderment and surprise he saw that the mountain was full of angelic horses and chariots of fire all around them. You see, to believe the impossible you have to be able to see the invisible. You have to position yourself to see things from God's perspective because the battle belongs to the Lord (Ephesians 6:10). God's perspective is never your perspective; He is always above any situation you encounter. My experience is that worship and prayer are inseparable, I will often cross over from one to the other and sometimes my prayers become songs and other times my songs become prayers. In this regard, worship is one of the key ways to enter God's perspective.

It is time to take the pressure off of yourself. You will not overcome the storm in your own strength. David knew this well when he confronted Goliath. He had seen what the Lord had done for him with the lion and the bear when they came to devour his sheep and now he was very confident that the Lord would do it again to the giant. Remember what he said in 1 Samuel 17:46?

"This day The Lord will deliver you into my hand and I will strike you and cut off your head"

We have to first believe the Lord will deliver the enemy into our hands before there can be any cutting off of heads. David declared to Goliath in faith what was going to happen before they had even started fighting. That is unwavering faith in the Lord who had come through for him so many times before. I always wonder if he was just a really good shot with the slingshot or whether, because of his great faith that day, the hand of God himself would have directed that pebble into the giant's forehead no matter how bad David's shot had been? We sometimes forget that Goliath was a very intimidating and scary person to most people, a literal mountain of a man who had put fear in the hearts of the whole army of Israel and their King for weeks. He had taunted them mercilessly day after day and created an aura of fear around himself. Yet when he came face to face with somebody who knew his God and knew that God would fight on his behalf, Goliath had no answer. Goliath was operating in the natural realm just like Elisha's servant Gehazi but David was operating in the supernatural power of God, just like Elisha. He had already seen the victory in the spirit realm which caused him to believe for the impossible in the natural realm.

It is so important to not only mentally understand this truth but have it written on our hearts so that we know, that we know that ultimately the battle belongs to the Lord who is in covenant relationship with us. If you are to overcome the intimidating giants in your life you will need to have this truth ingrained in your heart so that you can boldly proclaim in faith.

The Lord will deliver you into my hand and I will strike you and cut off your head!

"But I'm not a fighter, I'm a lover" you might say.

Don't kid yourself. The Bible tells us that we are in a fight but that the fight is not against human people (flesh and blood):

> *"We do not wrestle against flesh and blood, but against principalities, against powers, against the rulers of the darkness of this age, against spiritual hosts of wickedness in the heavenly places"*
> *(Ephesians 6:12)*

The "principalities" and "powers" mentioned here are rulers of darkness, spiritual hosts of wickedness literally hell bent on destroying you. If you are a Christian you are at war whether you want to be or not and whether you like it or not. Many Christians run around the battle field of life pretending the enemy doesn't exist while all the time the enemy picks them off one by one and destroys their lives. They wonder why things are going wrong? They wonder why they always feel sick and tired? It is because they are in a battle and they are oblivious to the fact they are being attacked. One of the most successful tactics of Satan is keeping the children of God weak and ignorant. In some cases there are Christians who do not even believe in hell, the devil or spiritual warfare anymore. Wake up! The Bible tells us that the devil prowls around like a roaring lion waiting to see who he can devour (1 Peter 5:8). I am not trying to glorify the devil or create fear because I know we have the victory over him through the finished work of Jesus on the cross, and at His Name every knee must bow. I am merely pointing out that we are in a battle, it's real, we need to fight and we need to know how to fight and not be ignorant of the devil's plans and schemes to destroy us (2 Corinthians 2:11). Only in the church do we send out troops to war with no protection, no training, no strategy and many times no idea that they are even entering the battlefield. It is time to lift the curtain on the lies of the devil and see what is going on behind the scenes in the spiritual realm.

We can see from the story of Daniel and many other places in Scripture that the battle in the spiritual realm is very real. In Daniel chapter 10, he is troubled by a vision he has seen and goes into three weeks of prayer and fasting to find out what it means for his people. As a result of his prayers an angel eventually arrives with the explanation of the vision which involves the overthrow of the Persian empire. The angel explains that the reason it took him so long to get there was because he had been fighting with the "Prince of Persia" – an evil territorial spirit governing the physical realm of Persia. This spirit did not want Daniel to receive the information from the angel and tried its best to prevent the angel getting the message to Daniel, until the angel Michael came to help. It reminds me of code-breakers in the second world war who would try to intercept messages from one part of the army to the other. This proves to me that demons and dark spiritual powers operating in the spiritual realm have a strong interest in affecting the outcome of events in the physical world. The same is true of your life and spiritual walk on this earth. The Holy Spirit is here to guide you into all truth but there are spiritual powers of darkness that very much want to adversely affect your life. You have the victory over them in Jesus name!

There are times to sit at the feet of Jesus and gaze at his beauty but there are also times to go to war and declare his authority over the storms in your life. Jesus is a lover but he is also the Lion of the tribe of Judah, and commander of the armies of the Lord...

"The Lord is a warrior, The Lord is his name"
Exodus 15:3

"The Lord will go forth like a warrior, he will arouse his zeal like a man of war, he will utter a shout, yes, he will raise a war cry, he will prevail against his enemies"
Isaiah 15:3

"Who is this King of Glory? The Lord strong and mighty, the Lord mighty in battle"
Psalm 24:8

I remember many times in my life when God has fought my battles for me. I just had to step out in faith and trust him. He is a good, good Father.

So what has this all got to do with praise and worship?

Everything!

When we lift up the Name of Jesus He is enthroned upon our praises and the devil is dethroned and defeated. When we worship Him even in the midst of adversity, great power is released and our worship becomes like a sword in our hand (Psalm 149:6). There is something so powerful about a tear-stained worshipper of Jesus. When we choose to worship God and not blame him or feel bitter about our situation it moves the heart of Heaven and gives angels flight. When we declare and decree things during worship, all of Heaven shouts in agreement with us and there is a shift in the atmosphere. That is what we will be looking at in the next chapter; the power of praise to shift the atmosphere.

CHAPTER 3

High Praises

"Let the high praises of God be in their mouth and a
two edged sword in their hand!"

Psalm149:6

One of the most powerful weapons we have at our disposal is to praise God with all our might, particularly in times of adversity. The devil cannot stand authentic, heart-felt, extravagant praise. The Bible promises us that God is actually "enthroned" on the praises of his people (Psalm 22:3) but let's be honest, sometimes it's the last thing we want to do when all around us is falling apart. It is actually an act of war on Satan and his kingdom of darkness when we choose to worship during adversity because we dethrone him and enthrone God who is the higher power.

When you feel depressed, when you feel hopeless, when you feel empty and numb, often the last thing you want to do is give praise to God. Yet you must! You must praise him at the worst of times for no other reason than that He is worthy of our praise, no matter what our circumstances. Situations change in the atmosphere of extravagant and abandoned praise. It is an act of faith, a marker in the ground, an absolute refusal to be defined by what you are going through. David danced with all his might before the ark of the covenant and promised his scorning wife that he would and could become even more undignified in his praise and worship if necessary.

Sometimes you can be praising God through tears or just singing in tongues and thanking Him for his goodness and his mercy, and suddenly His presence fills the room. He cannot resist worship, it is like a sweet incense rising up to him. In 2 Chronicles 5 we find King Solomon and all the people praising God as the ark of the covenant was brought into the temple. There were cymbals, stringed instruments, harps and a hundred and twenty priests blowing trumpets and praising God. It must have been quite a sight and the volume would have been piercing! They came to a place in praise where they were "as one" – that is the "High Praises" of God. As one they lifted their voices and sang:

"For he is good, for his mercy endures forever"
2 Chronicles 5:13

God could not resist such a beautiful unified chorus of people all lifting him up as one. The Bible tells us that suddenly the temple was filled with a cloud of God's glory. It was so powerful and so holy that the priests could not continue ministering in that place! Oh, I long for the day when we are so caught up in worship that the glory of God fills our churches, our bedrooms, our workplaces, our lives! I long for the day when the order of service is thrown out of the window because the cloud of God's glory is in the place and the ministers cannot go about their regular duties because they are flat on their face in worship and honour to God. Our services, our prayer times and our private devotional and worship times have all become too predictable. What would happen if you were to shut your bedroom door, put on some worship music and abandon yourself in extravagant, wild, unfettered devotion and praise to God? What would change in your life and how many of the things that you felt were so pressing and important would just fade into insignificance in His glorious presence? The glory of God needs to fill the temple once again. That temple is your heart!

> "Turn your eyes upon Jesus
> Look full in his wonderful face
> And the things of earth will grow strangely dim
> In the light of his glory and grace"

I know there are many specific Hebrew names for praise like *Halal, Tehillah* and *Ruwa* and they do make for a fascinating study – but when it comes down to it, you just need to throw your arms in the air, focus on Jesus in your heart and start dancing and praising with all your might! I could show you scripture after scripture where praising him loudly and dancing in his presence is mentioned, but at the end of the day it's not a formula or a prescription, it's a heart thing and once your heart starts beating faster and faster you can't help but throw your hands in the air and give God praise. Why is it that so many of us have no problem shouting and demonstrating passion at football matches and concerts but when it comes to God we suddenly turn into the 'frozen chosen'? It's not even up for debate! Loud, passionate, wild praise is all over the Bible; it's going to be loud in heaven so let's start practicing now!

"But I'm not a loud, demonstrative person," you say, "I'm an introvert"

Psalm 47:1 "Oh, clap your hands, all you peoples! Shout to God with the voice of triumph!"

It's not about whether you are extrovert or introvert, it's about whether your heart is on fire for God. Some of the most extravagant worshippers I know are introverts, including me. I am naturally quite reserved and conservative in normal life but when the fire takes hold of me I have to shout, I have to put my hands up in praise, I (sometimes) dance although I'm a terrible dancer.

When we authentically demonstrate that kind of praise coupled with the Word of God we go out to battle with a sword in our hand and God fighting for us. King Jehoshaphat knew this only too well when he went into battle. In 2 Chronicles 20 he is told that "a great multitude" is coming against him from beyond the sea. Does he panic? Does he run and hide? No! He calls a fast and seeks God. He admits he has no power against the multitude and he informs everybody that his eyes are on God; his faith is in God to fight the battle for him. Then God assures him:

"Do not be afraid or dismayed for the battle is not yours but God's"

v15

What did King Jehoshaphat do next? Did he make preparations? Did he hastily send out scouts to spy on the enemy? No. He bowed down with his face to the ground and worshipped. So what was God's great master plan to defeat this huge army?

Praise!

He sent the singers and people who were praising God out ahead of the army. Can you imagine being the enemy? You are expecting an army dressed for battle to come over the hill but instead the first thing you see are musicians and people praising God. It was to the tune of this sound that God brought the victory to King Jehoshaphat:

"Now when they began to sing and to praise, the Lord set ambushes against the people of Ammon, Moab, and Mount Seir, who had come against Judah and they were defeated"

v22

What were the ambushes that God set against them? He confused them to such a point that they ended up turning on each other and wiping each other out. Pretty cool eh?

Are you getting it? Praise is a weapon! You praise - God fights. When the high praises of God are in your mouth and the sword of the Spirit which is the Word of God (the Bible) is in your hand, you will defeat the enemy; you will overcome adversity in your life; you will be victorious. What does it mean to have the sword in your hand? I believe that when you praise God with your mouth and speak the truth of His Word (the Bible which is often compared to a spiritual sword) over your life a sword immediately appears in your hand in the spiritual battle to give you victory! When you sing verses from the Bible like:

"You are good and your love is everlasting"
"Your mercies are new every morning"
You are worthy of all praise"
"Holy is the Lord"

There are thousands of scripture verses you can sing and declare that exalt His Name. When you do it with a sincere heart of praise, He will come and place a sword in your hand for the battle. The problem is we have seen praise only as a touchy feely joyful thing we do at church on Sunday mornings. A happy-clappy song rather than a powerful weapon for the storms of life. Paul and Silas knew this only too well. When they were beaten and then thrown in prison they could have felt hopeless and given up but they didn't. They knew about the power of praise. Their hands and feet might have been chained but they still had their most powerful weapon; their voice. Think about it: we won't be sharing the Gospel in Heaven; we won't be praying, but we will be joining in with multitudes of angels in praise for all eternity! Praise is the closest thing we can do now on earth that lines up with what we will be doing forever in Heaven. It is a window into eternity. At midnight Paul and Silas were praying and singing hymns to God! Prayer and worship are so closely linked. As I said earlier in this book, I can sometimes be praising and suddenly I enter into prayer and intercession while other times I can be in prayer and suddenly burst out into spontaneous praise. Look what happened as a result of them singing and praising God:

> *"Suddenly there was a great earthquake, so that*
> *the foundations of the prison were shaken; and*
> *immediately all the doors were opened and everybody's*
> *chains were loosed"*
>
> *Acts 16:26*

They praised God and He set them free; He went to fight on their behalf! He put a sword in their hand. In Scripture you can see this principle over and over again yet we don't know it or practice it in many modern day churches or in our own private lives. Instead we allow Satan to ransack our lives whilst we exist in a weak and pitiful state. It shouldn't be so. This is a key to carry you through the storm and to give you victory in it. The power of high praise. When you turn on the light in a room, the darkness is expelled – this is the same principle: turn the light on, don't just shout at the dark. When you focus on the light and lift up His Name, the darkness has to leave because a greater power has been enthroned through praise.

> *"The light shines in the darkness, and the darkness has*
> *not overcome it"*
>
> *John 1:5*

"But if you only knew what I was going through" you might say "It's so hard, I just don't feel like praising God."

Let me help you. I have been a worship leader for over 20 years now and led hundreds of services. Do you think I "felt" like praising God every time I got up there to lead his people in praise and worship? No, of course I didn't. I had to make a decision that He is worthy of praise no matter what my feelings are saying: it's called a "sacrifice" of praise. Many of your victories will come from you deciding to praise God when your feelings are trying to tell you the opposite. It's a decision, not a feeling.

> *"In everything give praise; for this is the will of God for you"*
> *1 Thessalonians 5:18*

> *"Rejoice in the Lord always. Again I will say rejoice!"*
> *Philippians 4:4*

I will be honest, sometimes the sacrifice hurts and it costs. That's why it's called a sacrifice of praise: it will cost you something. Maybe it will cost your feelings? Your time? Your physical body may hurt and your legs ache, but we don't worship to get something from God, we worship Him because He is worthy of our praise and worthy of our sacrifice.

People sometimes say things like this after church services:

"I didn't like the worship today"

Let's be blunt, what has that got to do with it? The worship wasn't for us! We were not worshipping each other, we were worshiping God and sometimes that means making a sacrifice.

> *"Therefore by Him let us continually offer the sacrifice of praise to God, that is, the fruit of our lips, giving thanks to His name."*
> *Hebrews 13:15*

I remember recently turning up to a worship conference in America. I felt so alone and so deeply upset when I walked through the doors. The pain of my own circumstances had consumed me and I felt like I was in a dark hole that I couldn't get out of. I sat towards the back and just stared at the floor waiting for the conference to begin. People were nice to me and greeted me with warm smiles. I forced myself to smile back but inside I was dying. The band started playing and praising God. People got out of their chairs and began to dance exuberantly at the front of the church and in the aisles. I sat motionless in my chair, unable to lift my head. The weight of grief and despair upon me seemed to pin me to the chair. They were lifting their hands and praising God with all their might and I just sat motionless in my chair. After a little while I heard the still small voice of the Holy Spirit whisper:

"Arise and praise God"

'I can't arise,' I thought, 'I feel too low, too hopeless, too worthless'. Again I heard the voice encouraging me, almost like a whisper:

"Arise, warrior of God"

'I'm no warrior,' I thought, 'I feel broken and defeated'. I sat there for a little longer but then suddenly I felt something from deep inside me faintly start to rise up like a river...

"He is worthy, He is worthy"

A tear rolled down my face and I could feel the river inside me growing stronger.

"He is worthy, He is worthy" continued the Holy Spirit.

I slowly pulled myself up, raised my hands above my head and sang over and over.

"You are worthy God, You are worthy of my praise"

Tears streamed down my face and my voice began to crack but I just continued rocking back and forth with my hands in the air saying:

"You are worthy Lord; You are worthy"

Suddenly the grief and pain I had been feeling began to lift and it was as if I had a sword in my hand. My confidence began to return and the warrior in me began to rise up. I began to laugh whilst still singing "You are worthy". My laughter turned into warfare and I began to declare the truth of God over my life in agreement with His Word. Now God was talking to me and showing me things in the spiritual realm, plans He had for me and the amazing things He thinks about me. I went on to have a wonderful time of praise and worship and a truly life-changing conference.

Can you see the power of praise? Can you see that no matter what you are feeling you need to push past your feelings and just begin to praise God right where you are at. He will come and fight for you; He will come and break open the doors of your isolation and loneliness; He will break the chains of your addiction; He will fight for your marriage, your business, your health, your family, your destiny! He will bring you victory in the midst of your storm whatever shape it takes. Don't listen to your feelings, don't listen to the devil, don't listen to depression. The Holy Spirit is whispering to you right now.

"Arise mighty warrior, lift up your hands and praise God with all your might for he is worthy!"

CHAPTER 4

The Secret Place

"Whoever believes in me, as Scripture has said, rivers
of living water will flow from within them."
John 7:38

Years ago when I first became a Christian I was invited to a small
tent mission in a very small village in Essex. I didn't know it at the
time but this mission would change the way I viewed Christianity
forever. It was the kind of village that had cricket games on the
village green on Sunday afternoons – a sleepy little hamlet. There
were only twelve houses in the whole village and we set up our
mission tent right on the green next to the little church that had
invited us.

At this time I was a sort of punk rocker so I walked around in a
biker jacket, big boots and sometimes wore eyeliner – hardly your
conventional Christian. My official job was to guard the mission
tent from being vandalised by the local teenage delinquents.
I had to sleep in the tent overnight just in case they came while
everybody was asleep. As it happens they did end up paying me
a visit on the first night! However instead of having a punch-up
we talked until the early hours about God, life and the universe
while sharing a few beers along the way, and I ended up inviting
them to the opening meeting which was due to take place the
following evening.

The next day when the meeting started I am not sure any of
the twenty or so people gathered there were prepared for what was
to follow. The music started up and for a short time everything

seemed like a normal church service. I noticed some people yawning, others joined in passionately singing along with the solitary keyboard player as he launched into another chorus. I couldn't say there was a massive expectation from me that anything special was going to happen. In fact as I looked around at the few old ladies and families from the village who had gathered mingled with the smell of the old marquee, I distinctly remember thinking "Oh boy, this is going to be a very long week".

But....

Suddenly, from seemingly out of nowhere, there was a moment. A moment when it felt like God walked into the room in power and everything changed. The pastor could not stand because the presence of God was so thick in the tent that his legs gave way – we actually had to carry him home on a chair at the end of the meeting. The preacher could not physically see and had to be led around to minister to people because a glory cloud was in front of him. It seemed that everybody he touched was either healed or amazed at the words of knowledge that came out of his mouth. Some people were crying, some laughing, some declaring their secret sins publicly and demons were being cast out of people. Everybody was affected, including me. I just stood, wide-eyed, as my paradigm of who I thought God was and what religion and church were all about shifted in an instant. I knew I would never be able to go back to "normal" church again after this.

My newly acquired teenage delinquent friends turned up halfway through the meeting and were instantly blown away by the presence of God. Some of them became Christians that night. By the end of the week the tent was packed. Car-loads of people started coming in from the surrounding villages and towns as they heard about the miraculous things God was doing in that place. God had walked into the room that first night and that little church would never be the same.

There is something about the heightened change in the atmosphere when the manifest presence of God fills a room and all of the religious plans of men fall to the floor. The set list is thrown away, the sermon gets scrapped and all anybody can do is simply worship the King of Kings and jump into the river of His presence.

It was my experience of this presence at that little Gospel crusade that caused me to pursue God like never before. I wanted to know how to live in his presence and spend time with Him. I didn't want that presence to be confined to meetings and conferences. His presence is what I long for, it is what I love more than anything else because I have discovered that everything flows out of being in His presence and communing with Him. Isn't it true that when you love somebody, you love to be in their presence? I call that the *Secret Place*: the place where you go to be alone with God. I realise that as Christians we have the presence of God living in us all of the time wherever we go because we are now the temple or dwelling place of the Holy Spirit so I am not suggesting that we go in and out of his presence. I am suggesting that there is a difference between knowing by faith that his presence continually dwells in us, and experiencing his manifest presence. The manifest presence of God is different; it is the thick, weighty, discernible presence of God often called the "Shekinah" glory which King Solomon and his people experienced in 2 Chronicles 5 when the presence of God was so thick in the temple, the priests could not perform their normal duties. All the people could do was declare:

> *"For he is good,*
> *For His mercy endures forever"*
> *2 Chronicles 5:13*

Signs, wonders and miracles are often the evidence of a life cultivated in the intimacy of the secret place with God rather than the goal itself. When we make knowing God our ultimate pursuit in life we will naturally walk in his supernatural power. When I looked back over Scripture and particularly the life of Jesus on earth, I could see over and over again that He would leave the crowds behind and seek out a place where He could be with God alone. Everything Jesus did in public flowed out of His secret, intimate relationship with His Father. All the miracles, signs and wonders that accompanied Him during His time on earth were birthed in that relationship. I also studied many of the great men and women of God from the past (e.g. Wigglesworth, Kuhlman) and found that the secret of the power they operated in was their intimate relationship with God. All of the revivals we have witnessed on this earth were first birthed in the secret place. It is not enough to only pursue signs, wonders and miracles, we need to know Him, the source of all life.

I truly believe we are entering into a new move of God in which intimacy with him will be a primary focus because everything else flows out of intimacy. I believe the way that the Church operates will look very different in the days ahead and we will need to adapt as our old ways of doing things are challenged. It will be more essential than ever in this season to be in tune with God's voice and understand how to know Him personally. The experience of many Christians is only services, programs, conferences and the mechanics of church life. They need to be shown how to hear God's voice for themselves and cultivate that intimate relationship with him. The veil has been torn in two, we all have access to the throne room of God now, we do not need to consult priests and pastors to hear God, we are all priests unto God if we belong to Jesus Christ. Does that mean we do away with the pastors, preachers, prophets, teachers and apostles? Absolutely not! The five-fold ministry gifts (as listed in Ephesians 4) have a vital role to play in equipping the saints for the work of the ministry. I'm simply saying we need to be self-feeders, cultivating a strong inner life from our own personal walk with God in the secret place, rather than continually living on the revelation of others.

The Bible speaks of a great falling away in the last days (2 Thessalonians 2:3). I believe many of these people who fall away will be the 'Sunday Christians' who, when their faith is tested, will find that they have no relationship with God and no river to draw from in order to overcome adversity. When their services, programs, social events, sermons and committee meetings are taken away they will collapse under the pressure of life without the scaffolding of organised religion to prop up their faith. Please don't misunderstand me, I am not against meetings or events, in fact as a worship leader I love gathering together with the Body of Christ to worship. I believe the gathered church is essential to the Christian life. I just believe that it cannot become an end in itself, there must be an outworking that goes beyond the Church walls into every-day life and into the hearts of men and women.

Jesus Himself had this expectation of every believer; He knew the importance of the river of God's presence in every believer's life.

> *"Whoever believes in Me, as Scripture has said, rivers*
> *of living water will flow from within them."*
> *John 7:38*

Rivers of living water will flow from "within" them. Yet so often we are focused on the outward things in life. We are in a season of being called back into what is important to God. Relationship is so important to God; He wants an intimate relationship with you. The Bible starts with relationship through Adam and Eve and finishes with relationship through Jesus and his Bride, the Church. God sent his only Son to die on a cross and be raised from the dead just to restore that relationship with us. That's how important it is.

Recently I have been seeking God for direction and an understanding of what season we are in. God has shown me over and over again a picture of a tree planted on a river bank with its roots going deep into the water. The vision immediately reminded me of Psalm 1:3, and the same theme runs through Jeremiah 17:7-8.

> "Blessed is the man who trusts in the LORD
> And whose hope is in the LORD
> For he shall be like a tree planted by the waters,
> Which spreads out its roots by the river,
> And will not fear when heat comes,
> But it's leaf will be green,
> And will not be anxious in the year of drought,
> Nor will cease from yielding fruit"

What a beautiful verse. This verse encapsulates the very heart of what I am trying to convey in this chapter. We must let our roots go deep into God in the secret place. If we do we will be like a tree planted by the river that bears fruit season after season, year after year. We will not fear when the heat of adversity comes our leaves will stay green because we are connected to the source of all life.

Jesus would rise very early in the morning to go and spend time with God alone. He had such a close relationship that He only did on earth what he saw His Father doing in Heaven during these intimate times:

> *"Very truly I tell you, the Son can do nothing by himself; he can do only what he sees his Father doing, because whatever the Father does the Son also does."*
>
> *(John 5:19.)*

Jesus knew that the most important thing in his life was His relationship with His Father. It wasn't the miracles, it wasn't the popularity, it wasn't the power, it wasn't even His relationship with his family. Everything Jesus did in His life flowed out of the relationship He had with His Father in the Secret Place. In John 15

Jesus gives us the ultimate key to a fruitful Christian life of power and breakthrough with one simple word:

Abide.

He is the vine and we are the branches. If we abide in the vine we will bear much fruit. If we abide in the vine we will ask what we desire and it will be done for us because our will will be perfectly aligned with His. Without Him we can do nothing. It glorifies God when we bear much fruit and live a victorious Christian life. The secret is to abide in Christ. What does it mean to abide in Him? Spend time with Him in prayer, spend time reading and studying His Word, spend time worshipping Him, spend time talking to Him and sharing every part of our lives with him. Abide in Him, remain in Him all through the day, every day.

Let's be people who truly seek first the Kingdom of God and get into the secret place with our Father and let everything else come a very distant second. That is the number one secret to overcoming the storm in your life because when you know Him, you know His voice and you know He fights for you when you trust Him in faith. That confidence in Him comes from your relationship with Him and causes you to worship Him at a much deeper level. You do not know what tomorrow holds but you know who holds tomorrow.

Now that we have learnt the importance of the secret place it's time to crank up the volume in the next chapter.

CHAPTER 5

The Art of Shouting

"For the Lord himself will descend from heaven
with a shout"

1 Thessalonians 4:16

In the 80's there was a pop band called *Tears For Fears* who had a song called "Shout". The lyrics went something like this:

"Shout, Shout, let it all out
These are the things I can do without
Come on,
I'm talking to you
Come on"

Tears For Fears

There is a lot of truth in those lyrics. When you shout, you really do let out all the things you can do without. The years of frustration, the constant pressure, the failed dreams, the disappointment, the abandonment, the hurt, the pain, the broken things in your life. When people think of shouting it is usually attached to a negative image of somebody who is being abusive or has lost control but shouting can also produce a very positive release when done in the right environment and with the right mindset. For example, a simple study of primal scream therapy, a style of psychotherapy used to treat anxiety, trauma and stress will show it has been proven to produce a cathartic effect for people who suffer from pent-up stress. In that situation shouting is therapeutic and brings a sense of relief. How many times have you heard somebody say:

"I feel so much better now I've got that off of my chest?"

As long as shouting isn't abusive and is never aimed at a particular person it can actually produce a positive result.

It's also a very powerful way to declare God's truth over a situation in victory. Shouting causes a change of state inside you that enables you to move on and gain victory over the things that once bound you. It causes a release inside you and propels something victorious into the atmosphere that simply cannot be achieved by simply just singing songs or praying quietly. It breaks something.

> *"Oh clap your hands all you peoples! Shout to God with the voice of triumph"*
>
> *Psalm 47:1*

> *"So the people shouted, and the trumpets were blown. As soon as the people heard the sound of the trumpet, the people shouted a great shout, and the wall fell down flat"*
>
> *Joshua 6:20*

Shouting is very unfashionable in church culture these days and that's a shame because we can see from the verses above and many other verses in the Bible that shouting was used as a powerful weapon for God. Maybe that's why we have so many dysfunctional Christians, still bound up in the chains of their past, unable or unwilling to break free.

"That's all very well but God isn't deaf!" you might say.

True, but he isn't timid either and he isn't frightened of shouting, in fact shouting is all over the Bible and it is the way Jesus himself has chosen to return in glory. If it's good enough for Jesus, it's good enough for me.

*"For the Lord himself will descend from heaven
with a shout"*

1 Thessalonians 4:16

Yes, shouting is biblical and we see it in many places in the Bible. Something powerful is released when you simply declare and shout truth into the atmosphere. Sometimes shouting shifts something on the inside of you too that needs to be awakened, have you ever thought of that? When you shout from your gut, something shifts in the atmosphere but it also releases something inside of you.

Shouting can be a sign of war – when Joshua heard the sound of the people as they shouted he declared to Moses:

"There is a sound of war in the camp"

Exodus 32:17

The violence is not intended for people of course, it is intended for Satan and his demons, the spiritual forces which seek to destroy your life and everything you love.

*"For we do not wrestle against flesh and blood, but
against principalities, against powers, against the rulers
of the darkness of this age, against spirituals hosts of
wickedness in the heavenly places"*

Ephesians 6:12

I think many Christians will get a shock when they get to Heaven; I think it will be loud because many of the verses I read about heaven often say "with a loud voice". In Revelation 5 the apostle John sees a vision of thousands and thousands of angels, living creatures and elders all gathered around the throne of God. Suddenly he hears them shout with a loud voice:

"Worthy is the Lamb who was slain
To receive power and riches and wisdom,
And strength and honour and glory and wisdom"
Revelation 5:12

Can you imagine the scene? There will be no complaining and whining at the sound desk about the volume in heaven!

Now, do I think it is right to shout all the time? Absolutely not – as we saw in the last chapter there is just as much power in silence and intimacy as there is in shouting. Yet the art of shouting is something we have lost in the church. Shout! Break down the walls of religion and apathy that are trying to confine and limit you in the spirit. One of the many reasons I love King David is that he didn't care what people thought. He would express himself before God the way he saw fit regardless of who was watching and how crazy he looked at the time. I love the story about him dancing before the Lord with all his might even to the annoyance of his wife who sarcastically comments to him:

"How glorious was the King of Israel today, uncovering
himself today in the eyes of the maids of his servants, as
one of the base fellows shamelessly uncovers himself"
2 Samuel 6:20

David replies by reminding her that he was dancing before the Lord who had chosen him above King Saul to rule over the people of the Israel. He goes on to say that he will be even more undignified in his worship to God and humble himself in his own site if it brings more glory to God. Go David!

If we examine these verses more closely we find that David brought up the Ark with shouting and the sound of a trumpet (v15). Yes, shouting!

One of the most famous examples of the art of shouting accompanied by music in the Bible is the story of the destruction of the walls of Jericho. I have read that those walls were so deep and so wide that they used to hold chariot races on top of them – can you imagine the depth and width needed for that? You know the story: the city was shut down, none went in and none went out. Inside the king and all of his mighty men were waiting to destroy the Israelites if they somehow managed to penetrate the great walls. The children of Israel were facing what seemed like an impossible situation: locked out of the city with no possible way of getting in. That was until the Lord entered the picture and told them to march around the city before the Ark of the Covenant for six days in silence, only blowing trumpets – and on the seventh day they were to let out a shout at Joshua's command. Joshua ordered them not to make a single sound out of their mouth until he commanded. I believe this was because God knew of their capacity to complain and grumble and destroy the promises of God with their own negative and faithless confession cultivated from their years of wandering in the desert. On the seventh day they marched around the city seven times. On the seventh time the priests blew their trumpets and suddenly Joshua said to the people:

"Shout! for the Lord has given you the city"
Joshua 6:16

The people shouted and the city fell down flat. Just like that, a great city that seemed impenetrable was flattened by the power of God in one moment through the release of a great shout into the atmosphere! There is so much power released when we aggressively take in faith what is rightfully ours and push the powers of darkness back. What situation do you need to shout into? What situation do you need to declare and decree God's truth over in your life right now? It is the truth you know that will set you free.

Do not let Satan rob you of your destiny by staying timid and allowing him to ransack your life. Do not give up just because the situation seems impossible. Put on some worship music, rise up and start declaring the truth into your situation at the top of your voice!

You might say, "Ali, I'm just not that sort of person; I'm quiet, conservative and timid"

That may be your natural character, but don't tell me you wouldn't shout your head off if you saw some men pick up your children and run off with them and the police were nearby? Where would your timidity be then? You would run after them with violence in your heart and a determination to stop them in their tracks. Well, Satan is after your kids, your wife, your husband, your future, your peace, your family, your destiny, your health, your dreams and sometimes shouting is what sets you free from his grip. When we resist him and come back at him with the truth he will flee. The Bible tells us he roams around like a roaring lion to see who he can devour (1 Peter 5:8). Would you just let him do that without fighting for what you care about and love? Would you just stand there saying:

"Well I'm not that sort of person, I'm quiet."

No! When the situation demands it you would be loud, and often the situation does demand it because you are in a battle. Does that mean we have to go around in fear of Satan, being more devil-conscious than God-conscious? Absolutely not! We focus on Jesus and the victory we have in Him through His finished work on the cross. How do you get rid of the darkness in a room? You turn on the light; you don't complain at the dark. So when you are shouting you are releasing light into an atmosphere of darkness; you are declaring truth into an atmosphere of lies and despair. That is how Jesus dealt with Satan in the wilderness (Matthew 4) –

He simply brought the light of the truth of God's Word out against the dark and lies of Satan's temptations.

You will notice from the story of Jericho that the Ark of the Covenant went around the city walls with them as they blew their trumpets. The Ark is where the presence of God lived at that time; the covenant represents the promises made to Abraham and Moses that God would bless them and would always be their God. When we approach this aggressive warfare type of worship we need to be fully aware that the presence of God goes with us because He is inside us now; our bodies are the temple and dwelling place of The Lord. We also have full assurance and confidence that we are in covenant relationship with God. He is bound to us by covenant; He will never leave us or forsake us but He will always defend us, He will always keep His promises. We go to war in the presence of God and in faith we believe that He fights for us and is watching over His Word to perform it in our lives as soon as we declare it in faith over our situation. This is warfare worship, this is praise and worship being used as a weapon of mass destruction to the enemy and his plans.

I have had times where just to simply whisper prayers is not enough, or to gently worship is not what is needed. I have had to put on the armour of God and take my place in the battle knowing that the battle belongs to the Lord. There are times where I have felt so low, so defeated and hopeless that I've had to stand up and just shout for fifteen minutes straight just to change my state of mind before I can declare anything. Sometimes I go to a deserted field and just shout where nobody can hear me. I urge you to put on some stirring praise and worship music right now and give it a go. One album in particular has always helped me with this and it's from a man I respect and honour within the faith. His name is Rick Pino and the album is "Weapons of Warfare". That album has helped me win many battles in the privacy of my bedroom and my car before I ever saw the result in my life publicly. It is a divinely violent and beautiful album and it captures the heart of this chapter perfectly.

I will tell you something now that will really help you. You may be wondering if I'm one of those "shouty" extrovert people who just loves to be loud all of the time and loves to be heard above everybody else. The opposite is true. I am a very quiet introvert who loves silence and intimacy. I am socially awkward. I regularly battle with depression, sometimes for weeks at a time. I rarely feel like a victorious warrior of God and often feel like a failure. I am not some great prayer warrior of the Lord who lives in perpetual victory. Most of my victories have been when I'm at my weakest, on my knees with tears rolling down my face crying out to God. Why am I sharing this with you? I am sharing this because when the fire of God takes hold of this quiet, introverted, depressed failure, something happens and I turn into a warrior of God. I do it because I believe in it and I know the difference it makes in my life. If I can do it, so can you.

It's time to rise and declare the truth over your situation, it's time to shout!

"Come on
I'm talking to you
Come on!"

CHAPTER 6

Divine Violence

"The kingdom of God suffers violence and the violent take it by force"
Matthew 11:12

Let me make something clear before we go on in this chapter. I don't like violence but I do love breakthrough. I am as appalled as the next man when I see people physically hurting each other. There is no glory in that kind of violence. Like you I long for the day when we will all be caught up together in Heaven and every tear will be wiped away – there will be no more wars, no more sickness and no more death. However the reality until then is that we are at war with the principalities and powers of darkness and we must fight. That means divine violence in the spirit realm – and there is a particular strain of praise and worship which achieves that. Let me clarify, I am not talking about any form of physical violence towards another human being which is unacceptable and wrong. If you have been the victim of domestic abuse or any other form of violent abuse from another human I am not condoning that and I am just as appalled by that as any Christian should be.

The kind of violence I speak of is more of a spiritual attitude or stance in which a Christian aggressively pushes against the prevailing spirits of oppression, religion, passivity or other obstacles to break through into the victory God has made available to us in the spiritual realm. As mentioned many times before in this book, we are not fighting against people but against evil spiritual powers of darkness:

*"For we do not wrestle against flesh and blood, but
against principalities, against powers, against the rulers
of the darkness of this age, against spiritual hosts of
wickedness in the heavenly places"*

Ephesians 6:12

I remember the first time I experienced a shift in the atmosphere during a time of what I would describe as 'violent praise'. It was like we had broken through into a new dimension where anything was possible. I could feel the weight of my words as they flew out of my mouth like arrows and there was a kind of electricity in the air. These are the times when you are literally singing the songs of heaven; when you are literally creating the sound of heaven. It's a 'Kingdom-come' moment; a heaven-touching-earth moment where you can see what is happening in the invisible realm and as you declare it on the earth you see breakthrough happen. I was leading worship in a service recently when this happened. We went into a violent time of praise which felt warlike in style: minor key, lots of loud drums, very loud volume, almost tribal. All the religious spirits operating in people came out to complain as they tend to do when anything is happening under the anointing of The Holy Spirit (religion will always try and quench what God is doing, a religious spirit will always try and stop it). We had to be aggressive against the prevailing religious spirits that were trying to shut the meeting down. I started shouting "Signs, wonders, miracles" over and over as the song developed because they were the words I could see in the spirit flashing up like a neon sign. After a while I saw a picture of a wall being smashed to pieces again in my spirit so I simply began shouting what I'd seen at the top of my voice:

"Breakthrough, breakthrough, breakthrough, breakthrough!"

In the spirit realm (the invisible place we discussed in previous chapters where God operates and the spirits of darkness operate),

I could see heaven opening and touching earth, the atmosphere became charged with power and we broke through into a new place in the spirit, a peaceful place. In this atmosphere we began to play a Jesus Culture song called "Come away with me". The song speaks of hope and of God having a plan for your life; it talks of it not being too late for you and that the plan God has for you is going to be wild and full of Him. From the first note my stance inside was that the battle belongs to the Lord who would heal the pain, hurt, sickness, oppression, depression and broken dreams of people in the room. During the song many people came up to the front of the hall for healing and there were many testimonies of people who were healed during that worship time, some of them had been sick or in pain for years, some even had bones healed in that beautiful, intimate atmosphere.

Can you see how breaking through in violent warfare praise led to healing and intimacy? In my experience it is often the case that violent times of breaking through in warfare praise often lead to times of healing and intimacy in God's presence. It is almost like going on a treasure hunt. God has beautiful treasures available to us in the spirit realm like healing, peace, wholeness, salvation, forgiveness, freedom from oppression, depression, financial problems, marital problems and so on. The violent praise clears away the obstacles in the way of discovering them which are often spirits like oppression, intimidation, religion, apathy, condemnation and so on. In this scenario violence becomes divine, it becomes an instrument of deliverance and victory over darkness.

It is time to hear words like warfare, violence, shout and war in the church again. I know that's not very fashionable at the moment but maybe that's why so many good people are being ransacked by the enemy on a daily basis? They don't know how to fight in the spirit. We need to learn again how to go to war in our prayer closet, we need to learn again how to declare and decree with our mouths the victory we have over Satan in our praise and worship.

Do you not know that life and death is in the power of the tongue?
Proverbs 18:21

When we speak the truth and promises of God, things happen in the spirit realm. Life as God intended it is released. When we shout, it is like a divine atomic bomb going off in the spirit realm causing demons to flee in all directions. There is a shift in the atmosphere and God's Kingdom is further established here on earth. The universe itself was spoken into existence through the power of words. Just look through the book of Genesis, every time God says "let there be" into the atmosphere, Boom! It manifested in the physical realm. When we declare and decree the truth of the Word of God (The Bible) over our lives and into the atmosphere, all of Heaven is in agreement with us and God watches over His word to see it manifest on the earth.

"The Lord said to me, "You have seen correctly, for I am watching to see that my word is fulfilled"
Jeremiah 1:12

When we violently declare the truth of God in praise and worship over the lies of Satan, God watches over those words to fulfil them. Words are like containers of power and that is why when we declare them and sing them in warfare praise we can witness breakthrough in whatever situation we are going through. The Word of God (The Bible) is described as "The sword of the spirit" it is able to get to the root of the matter. Isn't it interesting that the word of God is described as a weapon of warfare? We need to use that sword when we engage in warfare praise along with the rest of the armour of God.

44

"Therefore put on the full armour of God, so that when the day of evil comes, you may be able to stand your ground, and after you have done everything, to stand"

Ephesians 6:13

"Take the helmet of salvation and the sword of the Spirit, which is the word of God"

Ephesians 6:17

"For the word of God is alive and active. Sharper than any double edged sword, it penetrates even to dividing soul, and spirit, joints and marrow, it judges the thoughts and attitudes of the heart"

Hebrews 4:12

Satan dreads the day when Christians will actually believe they are who the Bible says they are and they can do what the Bible says they can do through Christ Jesus. It's time to wake up. The Church has been like a sleeping giant for years, unaware of it's potential, obliviously asleep whilst Satan runs riot through the nations. A great awakening is upon us right now and the army is arising and taking its place in the great battle for the first time in years!

When I was younger I used to play rugby. I used to love the moment where the ball was thrown to me and I could run through people to get over the line and put the ball down for a try. I loved it because it would involve absolute conviction and focus from me. I knew I would encounter violence on the way to scoring a try and that just made me even more determined. I could feel hands slapping on my legs as I ran through people and I would hook my hand under people's chins and push them over; nothing was going to change my one goal of getting a try.

This is how we need to be with God's Kingdom. We need to focus and pursue breaking through into the presence of God with violence and passion no matter what tries to get in our way, no matter what the prevailing atmosphere is, knowing that He is cheering us on. Have you ever been in a position where you want something so badly you are almost violent about obtaining it? I remember witnessing the shoppers literally treading over each other to get a bargain the first time we had a "Black Friday" event in the UK. It was a picture of pure greed, which isn't to be celebrated, but it was also a picture of pure passion, focus and determination to breakthrough. It was violent. Oh that we could be as passionate about the things of God as we are about reduced priced electrical goods!

In the song "Reckless Love" by Cory Asbury he talks about the all-consuming, passionate love of God in this way:

There's no shadow you won't light up
Mountain you won't climb up
Coming after me
There's no wall you won't kick down
Lie you won't tear down
Coming after me

Wouldn't it be amazing if we could pursue God in the same way and with the same violence and passion that He pursues us! Indeed Jesus' violent death is often described as "The Passion" a death that he went through because of his all-consuming love for us. A death God, his Father, was willing to allow because of his passionate desire to be in right relationship with us again.

"For God so loved the world that he gave his one and
only Son, that whoever believes in him shall not perish
but have eternal life"
John 3:16

46

We see this determination and single mindedness in the lady with the issue of blood in the Bible. She didn't wait for permission to pursue Jesus. She pushed through a big crowd and reached out for the hem of his garment. She was not going to let that moment pass her by, and nothing and nobody was going to stand in her way. She was a social outcast; ceremonially unclean; unfit to be touched or seen in public but she still did it anyway. There was a violent passion in her heart and a determination to touch Jesus. Imagine if we could be so passionate about Jesus that we cause Him to stop and say:

"Who Touched me? I felt power come out of me"

Luke 8:46

Can we make such a demand on Heaven that we literally pull power down into the natural realm? Can we have such a violent passion for Jesus that we cause Him to stop in his tracks? Yes we can! The One Who made the universe; the way, the truth and the life was stopped in His tracks because one woman violently pursued Him and made a demand on the power within Him.

One of the weapons that I use aggressively in breaking through the enemy's warfare and entering the presence of God is the weapon of singing in tongues. I would say I use this weapon more than any other weapon I have in my arsenal. The Bible teaches us that when we pray in tongues we speak "mysteries to God".

"For anyone who speaks in a tongue does not speak to people but to God. Indeed, no one understands them; they utter mysteries by the spirit"

1 Corinthians 14:2

I know that when I sing in tongues I am singing directly to God and very often the mysteries that I am singing cause me to see visions in the spirit realm. These visions will often bring me victory or take me deeper into God's presence. I remember many times where I have been too upset in my natural self to pray or worship using English words and I have just sung in tongues and allowed my spirit to communicate directly to God. I am totally unaware of exactly what I am singing but it often brings peace and assurance to my soul, and breaks me out of the pit of despair. Sometimes we just don't know what to pray so it's better just to worship God in tongues and that's exactly what I sometimes do in order to break through. If you can't speak in tongues yet don't worry, if you are a Christian just ask God to baptise you in the power of the Holy Spirit. If you are not a Christian just ask Jesus into your heart, acknowledge him as your Lord and Saviour, turn from your old life and start living completely for him and then get baptised in water and the Holy Spirit.

The Bible even tells us that we don't know how to pray as we ought but the Spirit himself intercedes for us with groanings that cannot be expressed through words (Romans 8:26). This is what happens when you sing in tongues: you are singing prayers to God and the Holy Spirit within responds with pictures, visions, groanings, Bible verses and many more things that cannot be said or seen by just speaking normal words in your native language. All too often for me, the singing will turn into praying and then back to singing again, then it may turn into declaration and then into prayer as I pray into a vision or Bible verse the Holy Spirit has shown me. Can you see how singing in tongues is such a powerful tool and a great way of getting your head out of the way (your carnal thoughts) so you can focus in on Jesus? We need to focus on Jesus.

Have you ever seen worship in this way? It is so much more than just singing songs. The weapons we use against Satan in the battle are not of this world, they are spiritual weapons given to us by God to defeat the enemy in the spiritual realm where the battle ground itself is often our mind and our thoughts.

"For the weapons of our warfare are not carnal, but mighty through God for the pulling down of strongholds"

2 Corinthians 10:45

The strongholds mentioned in the verse above are the strongholds of our mind. The passage goes on to talk about how we can take every wrong thought that comes into our mind captive and bring it into obedience to the truth of Christ. This is where the battlefield is: in your heart and in your mind. Satan will try and influence your thoughts by lying to you and bending the truth. It's one of his primary tactics to get you doubting God's truth. He tried it on Adam and Eve and succeeded (Genesis 3). He tried it on Jesus in the desert and failed (Matthew 4).

The mind is a battlefield, we need to use the weapons God has given us to fight against the enemy and his plans to influence our mind. Weapons like praise, worship, prayer, the truth of his word, tongues, faith, shouting and violently declaring his truth over our lives and over the storm we are in. The time for timidity is over, violence and courage to step out is what is required if you want to shift the atmosphere and take hold of everything God has for you in the spirit.

It's time for divine violence.

CHAPTER 7

In Spirit & Truth

"God is spirit and those who worship him must worship in spirit and truth"

John 4:24

Have you ever played hide and seek? You find somewhere to hide and the person seeking looks everywhere to find you: under the bed, behind the curtain, in the cupboard – the search goes on and on until they eventually find you. If somebody is seeking you it means you are not easy to find; it means they can't find you. The Bible tells us in John 4 that God is "seeking" those who worship Him in spirit and in truth. That means He's looking up and down the earth to see if He can find people who will worship Him in spirit and in truth. He's looking in the churches, in people's homes, work places and secret places. He's searching up and down the chairs in the church, across the seas, in the deserts and in the forests and jungles of the world. His eyes roam to and fro across the earth searching. If He is having to search and seek it must mean that people who worship in spirit and truth are quite hard to come by don't you think?

So what does it mean to worship God in spirit and truth? Actually, before we answer that question we need to ask another question:

What does it mean to worship?

The word worship in the dictionary simply means "worth-ship" which means to show profound respect, adoration and devotion. In other words, when we worship something we are declaring it is worthy of profound adoration, devotion and respect. When we worship God we are saying he is worthy of our profound adoration, devotion and respect.

"Great is the Lord and most worthy of praise;
his greatness none can fathom"

Psalm 145:3

In some areas of the church worship has been reduced to singing a few slow songs on a Sunday morning but the reality is that we should worship God in every area of our lives: where our whole life is consecrated and set apart for him. We put Him first and worship or honour Him in our finances, our relationships, our family, our job. We use our time and possessions to show how much God is worth to us. We worship Him with our time and our talents and gifts by making time with Him and using the gifts He has given us for His glory. Too often our churches can be full of people who forget about God the moment they leave the building. Worship is for life.

A short study of the original Greek meaning of "worship" as written originally in the Bible gives us the word "Proskuneo" (Strong's 4352) pronounced:

(Pros-koo-neh-o).

Pros means "towards"

kuneo means "to kiss"

So when we come to God in worship we are intentionally coming towards him to kiss him. Our worship is an intimate expression of our love, adoration and reverence for him.

As human beings we are designed to worship and often we end up worshipping things or people that are not worthy to be worshiped like footballers, rock stars, preachers, political figures or even family members. We can also end up worshipping our careers, our money, our families, our status, our ministry. We direct our worship anywhere except to the person it should be directed, our Heavenly Father. Only He is worthy of our worship.

Now that we have discovered what worship is and who it is we should be worshipping, let's deal with the "spirit" part of the verse we started with at the top of this chapter. God is seeking those who will worship him *in spirit.*

> *"God is spirit and those who worship him must worship in spirit..."*
>
> John 4:24

God is spirit. He isn't bound by a particular place or church service because one of His attributes is that He is *omnipresent*; He is everywhere all at the same time. The Samaritan woman in the book of John chapter 4 wanted to know why the Jews insisted that the only place to worship God is in Jerusalem while her people worshipped at Mount Gerizim. Jesus answered her by saying it no longer matters physically where we worship because God is everywhere - He is spirit. Think about that! He only connects with your spirit. In the context of a church service he doesn't care what style of music you are playing, whether it's rock, funk, jazz or traditional pipe organ music. He doesn't care if it's a full band or just one person on an piano or guitar. He doesn't care what the setting is, whether you are alone in a field or at home in your bedroom with no musical accompaniment, in a traditional church or in a contemporary church. He is more interested in connecting with your spirit. It is Jesus speaking in this verse and notice he says those who worship God **must** worship in spirit and truth. It's not a choice. If you want to truly worship God you *must* worship him firstly in spirit.

So what does it mean to worship God in spirit? Your spirit is the essence of who you are, it is who you were before you were born and who you will be for eternity. If you are a Christian you have a new nature, you have been born again and the Holy Spirit is living in you. Your old carnal nature was an enemy of God but you received a new nature from God when you became a Christian and your old nature was nailed to the cross with Jesus. It is from this new nature that you worship God as the Holy Spirit within you constantly worships him. The Apostle Paul puts it like this:

> *"I have been crucified with Christ and I no longer live, but Christ lives in me. The life I now live in the body, I live by faith in the Son of God, who loved me and gave himself for me"*
>
> *Galatians 2:20*

Jesus himself puts it like this:

> *"Humans can reproduce only human life, but the Holy Spirit gives birth to spiritual life"*
>
> *John 3:6 NLT*

The Holy Spirit leads us in worship, we worship through the power of the Holy Spirit within and it becomes like a fountain springing up inside of us that we cannot contain.

> *"The water that I shall give him will become in him like a fountain springing up into everlasting life"*
>
> *John 4:14*

> *"He who believes in me ... out of his heart will flow rivers of living water, this He said concerning the Holy Spirit"*
>
> *John 7:38-9*

Can you see now how worshipping in spirit is so much more than just singing songs from dry head knowledge in a church service or being worked up into an emotional frenzy at a event? Worship must be in the spirit, you must discern the voice and the flow of the Holy Spirit within and enter in with your whole being. There is a flow of the river of God and you must connect with that flow. Rivers don't flow in straight lines, they meander and twist. Sometimes they are fierce and other times they are still. There are rapids, waterfalls and quiet places. In the same way our worship must reflect the flow of the river of the Holy Spirit. Worship is not just singing songs to God or about God, it is tuning into the flow of the Holy Spirit within us and expressing our adoration for him in all of our life wherever we are and in whatever we are doing. This is worshipping in spirit and it's a million miles away from just singing our favourite songs on a Sunday morning. This kind of worship is spontaneous, it doesn't need a band, it doesn't need a worship leader, it doesn't need a religious service, it is a river within you continually flowing wherever you are and whatever you are doing.

As an experienced worship leader I have led many meetings over the years and I can honestly say that I have felt the presence of God more powerfully in some of the tiny little traditional churches when I've led than I have in some of the larger, more contemporary churches. Why? It's quite simple. The smaller churches had people in them who were completely surrendered to the flow of the Holy Spirit inside them and the result was powerful. They had come expecting to get into the river of God and follow the leading of the Holy Spirit. Conversely the people in the larger churches had come to be entertained, sing their favourite songs and go home. They had not come to worship in spirit.

I was once invited to lead worship at a large church where a move of God had been reported to be happening. The service was being streamed around the world and many people had even flown in from other nations to be in attendance and witness this "revival". I was expectant before the meeting and excited to witness how powerful it would be for so many people to be united in the flow of the river of God at the same time. Sadly once the meeting started and I started playing I could tell that the people who had gathered hadn't come to worship God at all, they had come for a show. I looked at their faces, disconnected, some yawning and looking at their watches and phones as if waiting for the "main event" to start once the worship music had finished. *Surely worshipping our Father in Heaven is the main event?* I thought. They had come to see a side show. To be honest I felt the grief of the Holy Spirit inside me. He wanted to flow out of them, he wanted to drown them in the presence of God; He wanted to refresh them and put a new song in their mouths if only they would connect with him in their hearts. Alas, it wasn't to be; we plodded on through the songs trying to connect and awaken them but time caught up with us in the end and the show had to go on as they say. There were no miracles, signs or wonders that night and to be honest, I'm not even sure God was there.

When you became a Christian your old sinful carnal nature was done away with and nailed to the cross. It was put to death. You were given a completely new heavenly nature which is the nature of God. This is where we get the saying "born again" from; you were literally spiritually born again. You have been made into a completely new creation spiritually speaking.

We don't worship God from our old sinful nature (often called "the flesh" in scripture), we worship him from our spirit (our new heavenly nature). Your old nature will always try and deceive you, it will shout down at you from the cross where it is nailed and try and tell you that you're too depressed, too upset, too angry or too sad to worship God. It will tell you that you are too tired, too sick, too bored, too fed up or too hungry to worship God. Your head will start telling you that it's too silly, too irrational, too illogical and a host of other reasons to keep you from entering in to the flow of the Holy Spirit. Don't listen to it, kill it! Instead listen to the small still voice of the Holy Spirit within you, He will always want to praise and worship God, he will always be in tune with God. It will be like a fountain springing up within you no matter how you feel or what you think. Worship in spirit.

The problem is, your old sinful nature is at war with your new heavenly nature and will always try to stop you entering the presence of God.

> *"The sinful nature wants to do evil, which is just the opposite of what the spirit wants and the spirit gives us desires that are the opposite of what the sinful nature desires. These two forces are constantly fighting each other, so you are not free to carry out your good intentions"*
>
> Galatians 5:17

The old nature wants to do anything but worship God. It's your old fleshy nature speaking when you hear things like:

"I don't feel like worshipping God this morning"

"I'm too tired"

"I want coffee"

"When does this service end?"

"I'm too depressed to worship"

"I don't like what the worship leader's wearing"

Satan will do everything he can to keep you away from the presence of God. When you decide to worship at home you will find that the phone suddenly starts ringing, the doorbell goes, you remember you need to go shopping, the bins need putting out. You are assaulted by a whole barrage of thoughts and feelings that keep you out of the presence of God!

Why?

The answer is because Satan knows there is freedom in God's presence, breakthrough is in the river and he will use your old nature to keep you out. Now I know we don't worship God for our own benefit, we worship God because of who he is but Satan knows that when you get into God's presence and pour your heart out in worship you will be blessed. Don't let your thoughts and feelings from the old nature keep you out, worship in spirit. Worship is a decision, not a feeling.

One way of looking at it is that when we praise with our head (old nature) we can be singing the truth but there is no revelation in it. When we worship in spirit the Holy Spirit breathes life and revelation into our worship and it becomes a two-way relational thing. As we worship in spirit He reveals more of His nature to us which prompts further worship and so on, whereas spirit-less worship can be truth but also dead – with no new life breathed into it.

The latter part of the verse we are looking at says that God is: "seeking those who worship in truth"

Many people believe it means that we need to worship in doctrinal truth as in singing the doctrinal truth about God. As you have seen in other areas of this book I think this is an integral part of worshipping God. We often need to declare the truth about who God is and the truth about who we are in Christ, to achieve break-through. There is power in the Word of God and Jesus is the way, the truth and the life. While I believe singing and declaring the truth about God is essential, I am not convinced that is solely what Jesus is talking about when he talks of "truth" in this passage. The reason for that is simple. I have seen many people sing doctrinal truth without engaging their heart in the process. Put more simply, it's possible to sing doctrinal truth and declare the truth about God without believing it in your heart. I see it in churches all the time, especially at weddings and funerals. The devil himself declared the truth about God when he quoted scripture while tempting Jesus in Matthew 4. Just because you are singing truth doesn't necessarily mean your heart is engaged and you are worshipping in truth.

Have you ever been in a church service where people are singing worship songs but there appears to be no emotion attached to what they are singing? It's almost like a Christian form of karaoke where the congregation sings along with the band or organ player but there seems to be no heart connection to what is being sung. They may be singing about the joy of their salvation but their face looks like a bulldog licking a stinging nettle. This happens across all denominations whether charismatic or traditional. That is called dead religion and it's false, it's a lie because the heart is not involved.

Have you ever been to a church service or event where the lights are low, the smoke machine is on and the band are pumping out loud rock music? People are jumping around with their hands in the air, crying, shaking and gyrating to the music almost as if they are at a rock concert and the band is playing all their favourite contemporary praise and worship songs. They are looking for "an experience", they want to *feel* the power of the music, they want to be caught up in the moment. Now I am not against emotions, God gave them to us to express ourselves but could it be possible that sometimes when we go to church services or events that we leave having not truly worshipped God at all? Maybe we've just *experienced* a great concert, a tingly feeling, a nostalgic moment. Is it possible we just got caught up in the moment but there was no heart connection to God in what we did? Jumping around and throwing your arms in the air isn't necessarily spiritual just as being seemingly emotionless and quiet before God isn't always dead religion. In this way we are worshipping the experience itself rather than God. I have no problem with loud music, smoke and lights, in fact, as a bit of rocker it's my preference but I do have a problem with the experience becoming the goal. I have no problem with experiencing the presence and love of God in worship, but again I do have a problem when the experience becomes the reason for worship.

We must remember first and foremost who worship is for. It is not for us. Have you ever said something like this; I know I have!

"The worship wasn't very good this morning"

Hidden in that statement there is a belief that the worship is for us. We didn't have a good experience, we didn't like the songs, the sound wasn't the way we like it, someone else is sitting in our favourite chair or the worship leader was wearing very off-putting green corduroy trousers.

Worship is for God! That means no matter how it sounds, no matter what the leader is wearing, no matter what songs are being played, the style or the quality of the sound or what you feel like you make a quality decision to worship God because he is worthy. Worship is a decision not a feeling. To worship in truth is to worship with all your heart, all your soul and with all your mind. That's the most important commandment according to Jesus. (Mark 12:29-30).

It means being present, sincere, connected, authentic, giving it all you've got and engaging. Some people worship with their mouths but their heart is not engaged at all, they are lying, they don't believe a word of what they are singing, they are not worshipping in truth at all. God notices when we don't worship him in truth and when we are just going through the motions.

"These people come to me with their mouth and honour
me with their lips but their hearts are far from me, their
worship of me is based on merely human rules they
have been taught"

Isaiah 29:13

God is no fool, He knows when your heart isn't in it and it makes Him want to spit you out of his mouth. Does this mean that God can literally *taste* our worship?

> *"So because you are lukewarm — neither hot nor cold—I am about to spit you out of my mouth"*
>
> *Revelation 3:16*

When the words are taken away from the screen at church can you still worship or are you lost without them? Do you need music and words to worship God or does it just spring out of you like a fountain? Churches are full of people going through the motions; Sunday Christians just singing their favourite songs and then evaluating the worship based on their experience. God is seeking those who will worship him in spirit and truth, with their whole being, from their spirit, completely engaged, completely connected, completely in love with him. If you want to overcome the storms in your life you *must* engage, you *must* learn to worship God in spirit and truth.

CHAPTER 8

Deep Calls To Deep

Deep calls to deep in the roar of your waterfalls
Psalm 42:7

Many years ago a large company that I worked for would have its annual conference which would often take us to some really beautiful places in the world. We visited Switzerland with its crystal clear air and stunning snow-capped mountains. We met Bedouin people in the deserts of Morocco and watched snake charmers in the dusty streets of Marrakech. We sampled the delights of Sorento on the Amalfi Coast and walked along the magnificent streets of Barcelona. In every place we visited there was deep culture, beauty and rich new sights and sounds to immerse ourselves in. No expense was spared. From beginning to end we didn't have to part with a penny of our money. In the evening a big party would be laid on where many of the sales force would be awarded prizes for their efforts over the year in hitting or exceeding targets. I actually won a car one year for smashing my target (more about that in a later chapter). The employees of the company used to look forward to the conference all year long, it was the highlight of the sales year. I didn't look forward to the conference. In fact I used to dread it.

Despite all of the beauty on offer, the chance to experience another culture, and the opportunity to really connect with each other in a deeper, more meaningful way, most of the sales force opted to stay in the materialistic shallow end of life. They took off their wedding rings fully intending to commit adultery, they drank so much alcohol some of them could hardly exit the plane on arrival! They talked mostly about the things they could see or touch like: money, sex, drugs, food, drink, clothes, jewellery, music, weather, their job, targets, etc... Rather than look at these conferences as an opportunity to connect and enjoy the beauty of God's creation they just wanted to get drunk and have sex. Many would arrive at breakfast red-faced, unable to look certain people in the eye. They were content with the shallow things in life, the trivial and mundane. In short they did not want to go deeper despite the invitation being presented to them. Was I immune to all this? Absolutely not! I was often just as disappointed to find that I had shallow parts too even though something inside me ached for something deeper.

I don't say this to judge them, but actually to admit that in some ways I am just the same. God calls to me from the deep places within him to the deep places within me. He offers me the chance to enter his presence and commune with him and discover the deep secrets of his heart, but too often I find that I ignore the invitation, content to stay in the shallows and find any reason to avoid intimacy with Him. I suddenly remember I need to cut the grass, I realise that I haven't checked my email for at least an hour, there's a film I suddenly desperately need to see, I'm hungry, I want to chat on social media or play computer games. I know that it would only do me good to be in His presence but my flesh works overtime to keep me out. Why do we so easily get distracted and seduced by the minutiae of life? We need to renew our minds and live in the spirit so that we will not fulfil the lusts of the flesh!

> *"And do not be conformed to the pattern of this world,*
> *but be transformed by the renewing of your mind,.*
> *Then you will be able to test and approve what God's*
> *will is, his good, pleasing and perfect will"*
> *Romans 12:2*

*"I say then: Walk in the spirit, and you shall not fulfil
the lust of the flesh"*

Galatians 5:16

I see the same situation in church. We can be quite content to splash around in small talk but often have little interest in going deeper. God is calling to the deepest parts of us, the very core of who we are, our deepest emotions, fears, dreams, hopes, battles, beliefs. He is calling from the deepest part of Him, His innermost being to the deepest part of us.

God is looking for a two-way relationship; He is looking to share the deep things of His heart with us. There is something of Eden in this concept: a yearning from God to get back to a time when he walked in the cool of the day with Adam and Eve. He wanted intimacy but they, like us, were tempted away by the flesh. So much of the charismatic Christian world is about what we can get from God rather than how we can give into a relationship with Him. Preachers urge us to give money so we can be blessed and become rich. There are whole channels and ministries devoted to self-improvement and becoming a "better you". There is nothing wrong with investing in yourself, but it shouldn't be your primary focus. We are often only interested in what we can get rather than how we can give. God is looking for deep companionship and relationship. True relationship requires commitment and self-sacrifice, words that are sadly lacking in the body of Christ these days. Can we hear God over the chitter-chatter? Are we even listening?

It is no wonder that God calls David "a man after my own heart". David knew what it was to pursue the heart of God. He had a two way relationship in which he poured out his heart and it would appear that God did the same. Interestingly, David managed to have this kind of intimacy with God hundreds of years before access was granted to God's presence through the death and resurrection of Jesus. I have often wondered how David knew some of the things he knew about God? The Psalms are full of revelations about the future and secrets that were not revealed to any other man. Maybe as David chased after the heart of God he discovered that God wanted to be found, and in the intimacy of the deep, God whispered secrets to him and revealed His hidden treasures.

The word "deep" carries with it all sorts of connotations: unknown, mysterious, dangerous, unexplored, dark, intimate, untamed, unconfined. I am reminded of the ocean and the undiscovered secrets and possible horrors that lie miles beneath the surface. The deep is the place where all sorts of business goes on that nobody ever sees. What creatures really live down there? Nobody really knows. What secrets are hidden there? With the exception of deep space it's one of the few places man hasn't managed to conquer and gain ultimate understanding. We are still asking questions and we will probably still be asking questions thousands of years from now about what lies in the deep. Yet God knows exactly what is there. His knowledge is incomparable, He created it all.

Maybe we have a similar response to the deep things of God? He is calling us into unknown territory; He wants to show us things that may fill us with awe and terror at the same time. We will not be in control, it may make us very uncomfortable. It could be dangerous, it could be intimate. We like to keep God at arm's length so we can control Him and put Him in a comfortable Sunday morning box. We plan our services that way. Nice and neat, works well with the coffee time.

Except.

God is asking for more than that. He is calling us into the deep where our worst nightmares are faced, where our greatest fears are overcome, where our greatest victories are forged, where our fiercest battles are won, where wonder and joy are found and where His heart is poured out to us like a waterfall.

I love the second part of this verse we are looking at:

"In the roar of your waterfalls"

Psalm 42:7

I don't know if you have ever been next to a large waterfall – the noise is deafening! I have stood underneath a waterfall before and allowed the water to rush over me. It was powerful. In a waterfall you could shout at the top of your voice and nobody would hear you. You have to just give in to its roar and realise it cannot be controlled. Sometimes it is good to lose control, to just go with it and see where you end up. We can live such pent-up emotionally constipated lives where everything is wound up so tight, sometimes it would be very therapeutic to just let go and allow the waterfall of God to rush over us and refresh us. To enter the deep we need to 'let go and let God'.

There are deep things within you that even you don't know are there: things placed there by God when he was knitting you together in your mother's womb. The person you have become now is a culmination of the experiences you have had throughout your life so far. You may have accumulated possessions, ways of behaving and doing life, coping mechanisms. You may have been hurt or let down many times. Maybe you have a great job and your identity is in that? Maybe you live your life through your children? Maybe what you own or what you have achieved is the sum total of who you are now? It wasn't always the case. There was a more innocent time before you were born when God knew you, the real you, just as you are. He looked on you intimately, smiled and pronounced:

"Beautiful"

Maybe who you have become is who you had to become to get through life? God wants to strip all of that away and get back to the roots. You didn't bring anything into this world and you won't be able to take anything out of it. Naked you came and naked you will leave. He placed dreams in your heart that are yet to be fulfilled, he placed qualities in you that are yet to be used. Why not get under the waterfall and let it all out? Stand under the rushing water and hear the voice of many waters calling you back to the deep from whence you came.

During the materialistic sales days that I mentioned before, God's voice never faded. Though I walked in the shallows of corporate sales I was never far from the waterfall and His voice. It's time to leave the shallows behind and once again turn our gaze to the deep river of God.

Ezekiel has a vision of such a river in Ezekiel chapter 47. He sees a river that flows out of the temple where God's presence is. A man leads Ezekiel down through the water and begins to measure its depth. First he measures 1000 cubits and the water comes up to Ezekiel's ankles, then he measures another 1000 cubits and the water is at Ezekiel's knees. Still another 1000 cubits and the water comes up to Ezekiel's waste. Once more the man measures another 1000 cubits and it becomes a river that Ezekiel cannot cross. It becomes

"too deep, water in which one must swim".

This is an invitation from God. How deep do you want to go? Are you content just to splash around in the shallows forever or will you go deeper? There are so many things God wants to share with you if you will only respond to the call. Secrets, treasures, dreams, visions, revelations.

We love the happy-clappy praise songs and the dancing around and shouting, but sometimes when suddenly there are no words and we are required to go deeper we can freeze. It requires effort, it requires sacrifice, we have to start swimming; it's a river that cannot be crossed without swimming. God wants us to completely give ourselves to the flow of the river, to completely submerge ourselves and live our lives from that place. We need to become carriers of the presence of God, Kingdom carriers rather than people who visit the shallows for an hour once a week and expect our lives to change. We don't need another "encounter" we need a full submersion! The deep is calling you: it's time to shut the door, turn off the phone, close your eyes and wade in.

CHAPTER 9

Joy Is A Force

"The joy of The Lord is your strength"
Nehemiah 8:10

I remember the day I learned that joy is a force.

I was leading warfare-style worship at a monthly event which was normally powerful, but on this occasion nothing was happening. It wasn't changing the atmosphere and seemed to have no power, where normally it would be causing a breakthrough of some kind. The more I shouted the less powerful it felt and the more I declared truth and cranked up my playing into a frenzy the less the atmosphere changed. I was just beginning to get frustrated when a young girl who was visiting got up and announced that she could feel joy in the room.

I wondered what an earth she was talking about? Didn't she know that this was a prophetic gathering where we were meeting to shift the atmosphere over our nation through prayer and worship? This was serious business; didn't she know that serious business requires serious warfare worship? Apparently not.

She began to sing about joy down in her heart and to my surprise the congregation suddenly come alive! She began to dance and laugh and smile and to my amazement the congregation began to do the same. It wasn't long before the heavy, frustrated atmosphere in the room had completely changed and people were singing and declaring and shouting things but with a big joyful smile on their faces. It was strong, it was just as powerful as the warfare-worship flow; it was the force of joy! That was the day I learned that the joy of the Lord is our strength and that joy is a force all on its own.

The joy of the Lord is not just about feeling happy. The joy of the Lord has the capacity to enable you to shine even in the darkest moments of life. It is an overcoming, all-consuming joy that doesn't originate in the soul but in the spirit. In short, it is a supernatural joy and it comes from God. Joy is one of the fruits of the spirit (Galatians 5:22) which means it is not something you stir up in the flesh by willing yourself to be joyful; it is a spiritual fruit that you exhibit when you walk in close communion with God because it is only in His presence that you will discover fullness of joy (Psalm 16:11).

I have felt so miserable sometimes, especially when depression comes to engulf me like a cloak. It is in those times that I push into the presence of God through worship and prayer until His joy comes and removes that cloak of depression from me as I boldly thank him for His goodness, His faithfulness, His truth and His promises over how I'm feeling. Let the force of joy lift you out of the pit. Depression has to bow down; despair has to run; hopelessness has to move out of the way for the force of joy. Joy comes from faith, or knowing we can trust in the goodness of our Father God even when things feel bad we know He hasn't left us.

The word "joy" is commonly known to mean delight or happiness, but from a biblical and spiritual perspective it is much more than simply feeling happy. Biblical joy is a force that comes from deep within your spirit. It's an inner strength that comes from the joy of knowing God is your Father and you are his child no matter what the circumstances are, He will never let you down. It is a constant force that can be tapped into by faith when you are feeling weak or down emotionally. It will lift you out of the pit of despair if you decide to embrace it by faith because it belongs to the Lord Himself.

"*The joy of the Lord is your strength*"

Nehemiah 8:10

His joy is our strength! How do you pursue it? By thanking and praising God in faith for His goodness and faithfulness no matter what the situation and by asking him to fill you anew with His joy. The force of joy has the capacity to lift you above the storm so that rather than being consumed by it, you are flying above it; rather than being its captive, you are its master and it has lost the power to drag you down. The storm may still be upon you but it is no longer in you. The circumstances may look exactly the same, you may even feel exactly the same in the natural but something powerful has come from deep within you that is elevating you above it all to such a degree that you are even able to laugh and dance in God's presence. It's a supernatural force that embodies the knowledge of God's goodness and faithfulness and breaks chains of oppression.

Here are some scriptures in the Bible that talk about the force of joy:

"Shout for joy to God, all the earth!"

Psalm 66:1

"Come let us sing for joy to The Lord, let us shout aloud to the Rock of our salvation"

Psalm 95:1

"The Joy of the Lord is your strength"

Nehemiah 8:10

"Rejoice in the Lord always: and again I say rejoice"

Philippians 4:4

"In your presence there is fullness of joy"

Psalm 16:11

73

I love the verse in the book of Habakkuk where the writer basically states that although every conceivable thing is going wrong in his life he will still rejoice and find joy in God alone. He is saying that he will not be swayed by circumstances, however bad, even if he loses everything. Nothing will stop him rejoicing in God. Wow! He knew the force of joy.

> *"Although the fig tree shall not blossom,*
> *neither shall fruit be in the vines;*
> *the labour of the olive shall fail,*
> *and the fields shall yield no meat;*
> *the flock shall be cut off from the fold,*
> *and there shall be no herd in the stalls:*
> *Yet I will rejoice in the Lord,*
> *I will joy in the God of my salvation"*
> *Habakkuk 3:17-18*

It's incredible to hear the testimonies of those who have overcome adversity through the force of joy. Jesus himself endured the cross for "the joy that was set before him" - that's the joy of knowing he would set us all free through his death and suffering on the cross.

James actually suggests that we should count it all joy when we fall into trials because it will test our faith which strengthens us and produces perseverance. Why is that a good thing? It's a good thing because when perseverance has finished its work, you will be complete and mature, not lacking anything (James 1: 2-3).

When you finally realise that you cannot do anything on your own and you are powerless to change your situation you begin to rest in God. You rest in the knowledge that no matter what comes your way in this life, God is your Father, you will know Him forever and He is ultimately in control. That should free you up! Take a big sigh of relief, give it all to God and let joy flood your being. That's how Paul was able to praise God while chained up in prison; that's how some of the poorest people in the world are often the most joyful because their hope is in God.

I remember meeting the legendary evangelist T.L. Osborn face to face once towards the end of his life. During his preaching that night he had mentioned the agony of losing the love of his life, his wife Daisy who had passed away a few years earlier. He mentioned the loneliness and how hard it was for him to travel around without her even though he was with his daughter. Here was a man who had seen millions of people healed and come to know Christ through his massive stadium crusades throughout the world over decades of ministry yet he was in deep pain. As I waited in the line to meet him and have him sign my book I wondered how his face would look when I finally got to meet him? Would his eyes be full of pain and loss? Would his face be lined with grief and sorrow? I wondered if he considered ministry a mere duty he must endure now that his dearest had departed this world. Maybe he was willing his own death to come swiftly like a friend that would finally take him back to her?

Finally it was my turn. I looked into his face, searching for any clues into his soul. The first thing I noticed was his huge smile but then as I moved up his face and gazed into his eyes it hit me. His eyes were radiating pure joy. They were sparkling like big blue jewels that shone down into his soul. I was taken aback. I'd never seen eyes like that before. He had a joy that could only be described as supernatural; it surrounded his whole being. He had a joy that could have only come through spending time in the presence of God because in His presence is fullness of joy. Although he was in the middle of a storm consisting of grief and loneliness, the force of joy was at work in him, bearing him up and energising him. The joy of the Lord was truly his strength.

Have you ever laughed so much you've wet yourself? It happened to me once back in my school days when I was sent to stand outside the headmaster's office. As he questioned me and my friends I could feel that they were desperately trying to subdue their laughter which made it worse. Finally I could hold it no longer and to the dismay of the headmaster I laughed until I cried and wet myself. He told me to go away and sober up as he obviously thought I was drunk.

I want to be drunk on the presence of God like that! I want to be so overcome with joy and laughter that I just can't stop. I remember during the Toronto blessing in the 1990's preachers would come to our church and just as they were about to start preaching they would begin laughing until in the end the whole place was falling about in uncontrollable laughter. The preacher wouldn't be able to preach, the band wouldn't be able to play, nobody could do what they would normally do because the glory of God had filled the place, just as it did in the days of Hezekiah when the Ark was brought into the temple (1 Kings 8). I think God was trying to say "loosen up" to the church during that Toronto blessing. Why so serious all the time? The kingdom of God is not solemn and serious all the time, the kingdom of God is righteousness, peace and joy in the Holy Spirit! (Romans 14:17).

God wants to turn the way you are feeling on its head. When you begin to praise him and lift him up you invite the force of joy into your life; when you begin to dance and lift your hands in adoration to the King of Kings you are creating a pathway for the force of joy! It just requires you to take the first step and begin to declare his promises over your life with thanksgiving for what he has already done for you. We enter his gates with thanksgiving and we come into his courts with praise.

> *"Enter his gates with thanksgiving and his courts with*
> *praise, give thanks to him and praise his name"*
> *Psalm 100:4*

Give thanks to him for all he has done and praise his name for who he is; by doing that you have already entered his gates and his courts. When we do that he will do his part, he will give you:

"Beauty for ashes, the oil of joy for mourning and a garment of praise for the spirit of heaviness"

Isaiah 61:3

We can be safe in the knowledge that he holds tomorrow in his hands and that he will never leave us or forsake us. God, who created the universe, flung the stars into the sky, told the sea where to stop, created deserts, mountains, planets, galaxies and all life wants to be your Father.

Begin to worship him now, lift up his name in praise, think about the good things (Philippians 4:8) and spend time in his presence and you will begin to experience the force of joy.

CHAPTER 10

Rhythm of Heaven

"You turned my mourning into dancing"
Psalm 30:11

I will be honest with you right at the beginning of this chapter.

I am not a very good dancer.

I have friends who are great dancers and they have told me of the power of dance to set you free in worship. They have told me of being healed whilst dancing and chains falling off of them as they danced in the presence of God. It is an area that God is working on in me, I need to loosen up!

Recently I was at a wedding and my friend asked me to dance. I sheepishly agreed and smiled awkwardly as I approached the dance floor. I thought to myself that at least the music wasn't too embarrassing. Little did I know that as soon as I set foot on the dance floor the music would change. I waited for the next song and then suddenly I heard it:

"It's raining men, hallelujah, it's raining men, every step I take"

I had a choice: run back to my seat in defeat or take it like a man and give it my best shot. What followed was a very awkward "dad dance" style that barely passed as dancing at all, followed by *Girls just want to have fun.* My humiliation was complete, or so I thought…

Out of the corner of my eye I saw a man dancing like a dervish as if his life depended on it. His legs were going in all directions, his arms were flailing around and he was caught up in the passion of his own particular and unique style of dancing. I envied that man. I envied him because he was free, completely abandoned to expressing himself through dance without a single thought of what people might say or think.

"That's how we should be in our dancing before God" I thought, feeling slightly convicted.

We should be giving him all the glory with every part of our being in adoration and worship. That man was a picture of true worship as it should be; unfettered, unconfined and free.

I know I have mentioned it before but I cannot help but draw the comparison between the man at the wedding and David dancing before the Lord with all his might. What must it look like to dance with all your might? It certainly isn't a dad dance or the old 'charismatic two step'. It would be wild, raw, full of emotion, intensity and focus. I am sure it would also be very beautiful at times. David didn't care that he was King, he knew there was a King higher than him and he wanted to honour him with his very best. He didn't care about his dignity or reputation. He didn't care about social convention or protocol, in fact he promised that he would be even more undignified than he was being at that time if necessary. There is something about dance that sets the spirit free within. It is a beautiful way of expressing yourself to God and the passion you have in your heart for him.

I love the film *Billy Elliott* which is about a lad living in Northern England where jobs are scarce and life is hard. He lives in the sort of place that smells of hopelessness and the prospects of ever doing something with your life are minimal. Add to that grim back drop the fact his mother had left and he now lived with his grieving father and older brother and the picture is very dark. His father and brother both work at the local coal mine and Billy will also be expected to work there when he comes of age.

Except Billy has a secret.

He loves to dance.

When he dances it feels like electricity flowing through his body and he disappears. All of the problems and the darkness of his life are swallowed up by the power of dance and he loses himself in the moment and escapes from reality just for those few moments. Billy goes on to get a scholarship in London and becomes a famous ballet dancer. The end scene is very moving when his father travels down to London to see his opening show. It is a production of Swan Lake. As his father patiently waits, the music builds and builds to a crescendo and Billy enters the stage from the wings and leaps into the air in a majestic moment that captures everything dance means to him. His father is reduced to tears as he watches his son be the person he was created to be.

Isn't this a beautiful picture of what God sees when we dance with all our might before him? When we express who we are and how much we love and honour him through dance is he not moved to tears? When we become who we were born to be it moves the fathers heart. He must look down at our stuffy services and wonder what happened to us? How did they become so stiff? How did they become so lifeless? He remembers us in more innocent days before our hearts got broken and became cold. He remembers who we were and longs for us to let that person loose once again.

"God's not like that" you say "He wouldn't dance around like that"

Are you sure?

> *"The Lord your God is in your midst, a victorious warrior. He will exult over you with joy. He will be quiet with his love, He will rejoice over you with shouts of joy"*
>
> *Zephaniah 3:17*

The Hebrew word for "rejoice" her#e means to "spin around under violent emotion"

The whole phrase "rejoice over you" basically means to dance, skip, leap, and spin around with joy.

So the actual translation is: "He will *dance, skip, leap and spin* over you with singing and shouts of joy"

Oh yes, God sings and dances.

The picture here is God as a mighty warrior spinning and twirling around with violent emotion as he joyfully sings over you. Wow! Could it be that when we dance before the Lord in our services, in our houses, in our gardens or anywhere else for that matter that God himself dances and sings along with us?

Are you beginning to see how dancing is a powerful way to worship God in the storm? It can lift you out of the pit, it can change your state of mind, it can bring freedom and release you from bondage or despair.

> *"You turned my mourning into dancing"*
> *Psalm 30:11*

It's time for you to dance in the midst of your pain and get it under your feet! Dance until you feel invisible in the presence of God and the cares and worries of this world are swallowed up in his glory. It will literally turn your mourning into joy and your sorrow into laughter. The book of Ecclesiastes clearly tells us there is a time to weep and a time to laugh, a time to mourn and a time to dance (Ecclesiastes 3:4) so get your dancing shoes on!

> *"Let them praise his name with dancing and make*
> *music to him with timbrel and harp"*
> *Psalm 149:3*

Many years ago I was the lead singer of a very energetic punk rock band. I remember the energy I felt coursing through my body when I danced to the music we played. It was fast and furious but I felt real freedom and liberty when I jumped up and down around the stage to the pulsating beat. When the audience danced with me it was magnified all the more and it felt like a giant army all caught in the moment, all in perfect unity. We danced with such ferocity and energy that steam used to come off of me when I sat outside on cold nights after the performance. Imagine what it would be like if the people of God started dancing in unison to the beat of the Holy Spirit as one in a glorious offering to God. Imagine if they danced with the same ferocity and abandonment as I used to at those performances and as David did before the Lord. What kind of power would be released into the atmosphere?

Unfortunately churches are sometimes more like the town in the film Footloose who outlawed dancing and rock music. They wanted to keep everything safe and controlled and crush any sign of passion, individualism or spontaneity. Some churches are like that. They would even consider dancing to be of the devil, unrighteous or just plain rebellious. It is no wonder then that people are literally voting with their feet and church attendance in general is on a very steep decline. The world looks on and sees the miserable religious faces, the passionless worship, the formulaic services and wants no part in it. They can go to a club down the road and have so much more fun. The world knows how to have fun because it isn't bound by all the religious rules of the church. What the world doesn't have is true joy and the wonderful gospel of Jesus Christ. They know how to party but that road leads to emptiness.

The people of God need to learn how to dance again, how to have fun again, how to *feel* again! We carry the most powerful message on the earth, the gospel of Jesus, a good news story of love, grace and hope. Surely we should be the most joyful people on the planet?

It's time to loosen up and be footloose and fancy free. I'm saying crank up the music and start dancing in your bedroom, in your living room, in your kitchen, in your garden, in your church service and let God release rivers of living water from deep within you. As the words of the popular song *Holy Ghost Party* by Cory Asbury say:

If you know the Lord's been good to you
If you know the Lord's been good to you
If you know the Lord's been good to you
Come on and dance, dance, dance, dance, dance
You know what to do.

CHAPTER 11

Forged In The Storm

"But those who wait on the Lord shall renew their
strength, they shall mount up on wings like eagles,
they shall run and not be weary, they shall walk and
not faint"

Isaiah 40:31

Smith Wigglesworth was an extraordinary man who moved powerfully in signs, wonders and miracles during his ministry in the early 1900's. He was also a man who was accustomed to pain in his health and personal life. He knew what it was to come through the storms of life. He knew that as he yielded to the power of God, he became stronger inside. It is reported that in one particular meeting when he lifted his hands to pray, the glory of God filled the room to such a degree that the other ministers praying with him had to crawl out of the room on their hands and knees because they didn't have the capacity to stand in such a presence. This man had surrendered himself to God to such a degree that he was literally walking in glory. He once said:

"In me is working a power stronger than every other
power. The life that is in me is a thousand times bigger
than I am outside"

Smith Wigglesworth

You can tell when somebody has been forged in the storm. They have a strength and a depth in them that others simply don't seem to possess. Those months and sometimes years of continuously standing in faith and believing when all around them is crashing down have cultivated an immovable faith in them like a rod of iron. The countless times they have poured out their heart to God in worship as the storm beat down on their lives have created an intimacy with God that very few know. When they worship, they worship with all of their heart, with all of the knowledge of the times God has fought for them in battle again and again. They know their strength comes from the Lord and they draw their strength from Him. They might be physically weak but when they step into the presence of God they mount up with wings like eagles

"But those who wait on The Lord
Shall renew their strength;
They shall mount up with wings like eagles,
They shall run and not be weary,
They shall walk and not faint"

Isaiah 40:31

They are a thousand times bigger on the inside than they are on the outside. They are not conformed to the pattern of this world.

"Do not be conformed to the pattern of this world, but
be transformed by the renewing of your mind"

Romans 12:2

They are not afraid of the storm because they know from experience that God in them is bigger.

They remind me of the palm tree which also does well in a storm. It has several characteristics that help it to do so which are very similar to those who have been forged in the storms of life. Firstly, its construction which looks like the inside of an electrical wire with many small strands making up the whole, rather than the circular pattern that allows conventional trees to grow wide and strong in rigidity. Why is that important? The construction of a palm tree allows it to bend in the wind whereas a circular tree snaps under extreme pressure. The palm tree's ability to bend in the wind makes it much more able to survive storms, often becoming stronger after the storm.

The great revivalist Evan Roberts who was famous during the Welsh revival of 1904 prayed:

"Bend me; bend me Lord"

He wanted to be conformed to the will and image of God. The result of his earnest prayers for bending was a mighty harvest of souls and one of the most powerful revivals of all time. Could it be that, like the palm tree, the more we are able to bend in the storm, the more we will be conformed into the image of God, and the more equipped we will be to withstand the storms of life? Could it be that as we learn to bend that we come back stronger too? That as we learn to worship in the midst of adversity we are cultivating a strength within us that can never be destroyed?

Another aspect of the palm tree's durability is that it has a very large set of rambling roots that are spread across the soil close to the surface. They secure the soil around the rootball of the tree and act as a heavy anchor. So rather than having just a few strong roots that go down deep it has many roots that help it stay 'bottom-heavy'.

"This hope we have as an anchor of the soul, a hope
both sure and steadfast and one which enters the veil"
Hebrews 6:19

Jesus is our anchor, he has gone before us, behind the veil in the Holy of Holies as our high priest forever, and has provided a way for us to enter in. Through his death and resurrection, Jesus is now our anchor in the storm! Just like the palm tree, we can bend in the winds of adversity knowing that we won't snap because we are anchored to the King of Glory.

Yet another aspect of the palm tree is that its branches, which are quite small, fold in with the wind in an almost 'feather like' way letting the wind pass through them, whereas the branches of other trees tend to act like a sail in the wind which causes the tree to be uprooted. The feather-like small branches of a palm tree fold in and help protect the tree from the storm. Isn't this a picture of what God does to us when we come to him and abide in him (John 15)?

> *"He will cover you with his feathers. He will shelter you with his wings. His faithful promises are your armour and protection"*
>
> Psalm 91:4

It is interesting how we have a description here of God who is sheltering us from the storm with His feathers while also acting as a shield and armour in the battle through his faithfulness and promises to us. If we can bend in the winds of trouble and allow him to be our anchor through his word, He will cover us with his feathers and we will be indestructible in the storm! Hallelujah!

The picture here is summed up very effectively in the beautiful Hillsong worship song *Cornerstone*.

> *"Christ alone, Cornerstone. Weak made strong, in the Saviour's love. Through the storm, He is Lord, Lord of all"*
>
> Hillsong

The verse also speaks of the same thing.

> *"In every high and stormy gale, my anchor holds within the veil"*
>
> Hillsong

In one of the storms of my life I was over £20,000 in debt and at the point where I was using credit cards to pay off credit cards. I had around five credit cards and they were all maxed out. We had four children and the rent to pay as well as all the other pressures that come with a growing family.

I'll never forget it. On New Year's Eve I knelt down and repented of stewarding my finances badly. I took communion and cried out to God for deliverance from the financial prison I had created for myself. As I did this I distinctly heard the Holy Spirit tell me to cut up all of the cards so that I could no longer depend on them. I tried to bargain with God and asked if I could just freeze them in our freezer so that I couldn't use them without thawing them out... just in case. God would not be bargained with – His command was absolute; I had to cut them up. I took a deep breath, cut the cards up and stepped out in faith.

What followed was three months of pain and hardship. I couldn't afford anything; we could barely afford grocery shopping, yet somehow provisions came in. I remember not being able to pay for the parking when I went to see my customers as a Salesman. I would have to find the nearest supermarket which had free parking and walk to my customer's office no matter how far away that might be. There were times when I questioned what I had done and a fear gripped me: the fear of losing our house, the fear of not being able to provide for my family, the fear of people coming and taking away our possessions. Letters and calls were coming in daily demanding the money owed. I would drive from appointment to appointment crying and worshipping to CD's in my car, thanking God for his mercy and grace. Every time I felt fearful I would pray and ask God to help me and the still small voice of the Holy Spirit would come and reassure me with a whisper *"Just trust me, just trust me"*

At the time there was a competition being run in my workplace among the sales force. The competition was presented in the form of a mountain that you had to climb. Each time you sold something you progressed higher up the mountain. The first sales person to the summit would be given a brand new Chrysler Crossfire car. I was quite far down the table when they announced the competition but something about it struck me. The fact of it being a symbolic mountain when I was believing God to remove a mountain of debt in my life captured my imagination. Something inside me decided that I was going to win the competition. The year was 2005. It was the best year I ever had in my sales career. I found some huge clients by pounding the streets, business parks and town centres and knocking on every door I could find. By the end of that first three months which had felt like hell on earth I was sitting at the summit of the mountain with just over £900,000 of sales! God had done it! I won the car and was able to pay off the entire debt and have some left over once the car was sold. God is so good.

The point in telling this story is simply just to say this: if you don't give up, if you persevere, if you allow God to be your anchor and your shelter from the storm, He will come and deliver you; He will fight the battle with you and for you. I was a different person after that experience. Suddenly there was a strength and steeliness about me that wasn't there before. I had worshipped God in the storm and come through to the other side; I had a testimony to tell. Unless you are tested, how can you have a testimony? Smith Wigglesworth puts it this way:

> *"Great faith is the product of great fights. Great testimonies are the outcome of great tests. Great triumphs can only come out of great trials"*
>
> Smith Wigglesworth

This is a word of encouragement to you for whatever storm you are facing in your life right now. No matter what you are going through, God is bigger and He is worthy of your worship. Trust him. Worship him and see him bring you through.

Remember that even if you are broken, you still have a song to sing, know that the battle is the Lord's, and that through high praises you can find that place of victory. No matter how defeated, dirty, beaten up or unworthy you feel, He loves you and will always be waiting for you in the secret place with open arms. Don't be afraid to shout! Don't be afraid to get divinely violent in the battle to get your breakthrough. Remember to worship him with everything you've got from your spirit and He will call to you from the deep places. Let his joy lift you out of the pit and let the rhythm of Heaven carry you to a new place of victory and freedom in your life!

Finally, allow God to forge in you a faith that cannot be shaken, a resolve that will not be broken and a fire that will never go out, for that is the testimony of those who step out on to the water and worship in the storm.

Printed in Great
Britain
by Amazon

32204923R00061